THE MAN WHO FELL IN A HOLE

by

C. D. Neill

Grosvenor House
Publishing Limited

The right of C. D. Neill to be identified as the author of this
work has been asserted in accordance with Section 78
of the Copyright, Designs and Patents Act 1988

The book cover is copyright to C. D. Neill

This book is published by
Grosvenor House Publishing Ltd
Link House
140 The Broadway, Tolworth, Surrey, KT6 7HT.
www.grosvenorhousepublishing.co.uk

This book is a work of fiction. Any resemblance to
people or events, past or present, is purely coincidental.

A CIP record for this book
is available from the British Library

ISBN 978-1-83975-175-2

Other books featuring Detective Inspector Wallace Hammond
Doors Without Numbers
Shoes on a Wire

****

For Ed x

'Nobody can give you freedom. Nobody can give you equality or justice or anything. If you're a man, you take it.'

Malcolm X

PROLOGUE

'It's a fact that over two-and-a-half thousand left-handed people are killed every year from using asymmetrical equipment designed for right-handed people.'

Dominic delivered his intellectual offering in his usual manner, with his head bowed, his eyes focused on the floor, his arms held at his sides, rigid and still.

Alice smiled. 'That is interesting, if a little negative, but since I am only using scissors, I do not think I am likely to be in any danger.' Nonetheless, she replaced the scissors in the drawer and sought an alternative pair. Not finding any, she resorted to folding the paper and tearing carefully along the folds. The slightly jagged edges of the name tags were sufficient.

She selected Dominic's name from the pile, scribbled a return date on the paper and turned to the trolley behind her, seeking the titles she had previously organised.

'If you were a starfish, you would be less likely to die from cutting your hand, because you could regenerate one.' Dominic continued the conversation, all the while avoiding eye contact but showing interest in her actions.

'I can't see a starfish being able to work here, though.' Alice was attempting to end the topic of conversation, but as usual her flippancy was not recognised as humour. Dominic was not a nuisance, but his conversations had a tendency to develop into a realm beyond the norm if he was given the opportunity. 'Perhaps it would be easier if I were multi-dexterous like Leonardo da Vinci.'

Alice turned away from the trolley and bound three books together with an elastic band, tucking Dominic's name tag underneath.

'I think you mean ambidextrous.' Dominic's voice adopted an authoritative tone. 'Leonardo da Vinci could draw with one hand and write with the other. You are sinistrous, because you tend towards the left. In some societies, you would be considered a bad omen.' Dominic paused briefly whilst he contemplated the notion. 'I do not think you are a bad omen. I think you are a good person.'

There was the sound of a soft chuckle being emitted discreetly from the mezzanine over-looking the reception desk. Alice flushed, aware that her conversation with Dominic was being overheard.

'That is a comforting thought.' She ended the possibly endless conversation and resumed her usual efficient mode. 'You won't be able to extend the loan for the first book because it has been reserved by another customer, so I've written the return date for you.'

She proffered the pile of books by leaning over the counter, and waited for him to cautiously step forward and retrieve them. Dominic returned to his original position in front of the counter and stood cradling the books in his arms. He had begun to rock slowly on his feet, which Alice understood as a symptom of his impending awkwardness.

She smiled reassuringly towards his bowed head. 'I will see you next week, Dominic. Enjoy your reading. I've got to close the library now, but I will have some more titles ready for when I next see you.'

Dominic, head still bowed, raised a hand towards the upper mezzanine in the library. 'Bye, Elijah'.

'Goodbye, Dominic, see you soon,' a man's voice called softly from the local history section of the library as Dominic retreated towards the exit.

Soon after, there was the sound of a scraping chair, a jingle of keys, then footsteps descending from the stairs adjacent to the desk where Alice was logging off the computer. Elijah, a tall, well presented man in his early fifties, paused by the desk as he put on his jacket.

'He's a sweet boy. You get on well with him.' He beckoned his head towards the door where Dominic had exited.

'Yes, he is.' Alice smiled shyly, embarrassed he had heard her being referred to as a possible ill omen. 'He's a walking encyclopaedia!'

Elijah nodded without answering, his notebook clasped between his teeth as he returned his pen to the inner pocket of his tan leather jacket. 'Oh well. You need to close, and I must not overstay my welcome.' He headed to the exit.

Alice watched him as he went out of the door. Her eyes clung to his retreating back, admiring the broad shoulders and toned limbs, willing the power to pull him back. Then she heaved a long, heavy sigh and went to lock the doors behind him.

Elijah Johnson left the library shortly after 6pm on the evening of April 10. He paused outside the door, noting that the sky had blackened since he had arrived four hours previously, and wished he had brought the car. The four-mile walk along the canal towards the town had seemed a good idea when it had been bright and warm, but now the threat of impending rain dampened his spirits as well as the air.

He zipped his jacket to the collar and dug his hands deep into his jean pockets as he ventured away from the public library towards the town. He paused for a moment on the main bridge, noting the crocuses were beginning to bloom on the canal banks. The hint of pinks and purples, together with the yellow daffodils, brightened the otherwise murky palette of the canal. Soon the willow trees would cascade green ribbons overhanging the bright blues of the rowing boats, as the influx of tourists arrived for their Easter holidays.

Hythe was a pretty town, in Elijah's view. It was not the most modern of towns, and lacked department stores or outlets of designer brands. But for many, the old-fashioned high street with the traditional pub, butcher, baker, and stationer's, were reminiscent of the days when communities flourished as a united population.

Elijah's musings were interrupted by an excited cocker spaniel sniffing at his heels. He smiled at the dog's owner, dismissing her need to apologise, and petted the dog for several seconds before making his way to the small supermarket near the square.

He bought chicken liver pate, a wholemeal baguette made with French yeast, and a bottle of pale ale for a quick tea when he got home. As he made his way to the checkout, he smiled at a couple he recognised from the leisure club, and exchanged quick pleasantries before remembering he needed porridge oats, so excused himself to search the next aisle. The checkout was fast, and he left the shop within ten minutes of entering.

As he made his way to the bus stop, Elijah considered whether he should have bought something for Mischa.

She was not due to visit today, but if she changed her mind, it would be nice to have something to offer. His pace faltered a little as he pondered whether to go back to the shop, but then continued ahead. If Mischa did turn up, he had enough to share; if not, a takeaway would be a nice treat.

He boarded the bus and automatically headed towards the twin seats by the emergency exit door. Elijah always favoured this seat, as other passengers tended to sit at the front or the back before the middle seats were taken, so his bus journeys were usually a brief respite with peace and anonymity. He was surprised when another passenger stood beside his seat and looked straight at him.

Elijah looked up with a polite smile, whilst attempting to predict the person's intentions. The face was unrecognisable due to the large hood that shadowed their features, creating an unformed shape. The bus had begun to move, yet the person continued to stand before Elijah, one hand resting on the back of the seat, the other arm holding onto the safety bar. Elijah shifted his weight towards the far side to allow more room for his fellow passenger, expecting them to sit down. There was no response. He began to feel uneasy.

'Do you want to sit down?' The awkwardness of the situation meant that decorum was less warranted, so Elijah now directly addressed the person next to him. The features underneath the hood were angular – a thin long nose; a prominent chin. The face was small, but male or female, he couldn't be sure. The mouth was set. The eyes were intent and fixed on him with evident hostility.

He flashed a look towards the passengers seated in front of him. A young woman was occupied with her baby in the pushchair before her, an older woman fussed with her shopping bags. A youth oblivious to his surroundings was nodding his head to the sound emitting from his earphones. No-one was behind him. No-one was looking in his direction. Elijah's unease was quickly escalating into panic.

Their exchange had been only a few seconds, yet it seemed a prolonged time before the other passenger sat down. The person's body slid onto the seat so that their weight pressed against Elijah. Then they moved so that their elbows dug into Elijah's flesh, and he glanced down. Beside him, the passenger had retrieved an object from their pocket. It was small enough to be concealed in their hand. Their fingers were clasped around it, but then their hand uncurled to reveal the silver point and serrated edge.

The knife was turned towards his ribs.

Elijah's mouth had gone dry, his prayer was barely audible. 'Please, no!'

*

CHAPTER ONE

'So, winding your neck in, eh?'

Detective Sergeant Peters addressed Detective Inspector Wallace Hammond in a discourteous manner, but it was absent of any malicious intent.

Hammond eyed his colleague with a resigned air and watched the man walk across the open-plan office, but said nothing in response. Instead, he turned back to his computer screen and continued scrolling through the CCTV videos of an exit route used by a white Audi A3 at the weekend. The suspicion was that the car used during a violent burglary had been stolen, changed to false plates, and since been destroyed. But it was necessary to check where the information could lead, and Hammond had been the obvious choice of team member for the task.

For the last three years, his expertise as a Detective Inspector had been somewhat ignored in preference for the younger, more enthusiastic and computer-literate detectives. Bit by bit Hammond's responsibilities had dwindled, until now here he was doing the more menial tasks normally delegated to those of a lower rank. Hammond was not despondent, though. With only four weeks to go until his sixty-first birthday, he was looking forward to retirement, hence the jibes from his colleagues.

There had been a time when the thought of retiring had repelled Hammond, particularly after his divorce from Lyn, when the thought of having nothing to occupy his mind or his time was frightening. He had heard of former colleagues turning to gardening as an outlet for their energy, but Hammond had enough difficulty just distinguishing a weed from a wild flower. Recently he had seen a former police commissioner feature in *British Bake Off*, having switched careers to become a pâtissier. Whilst Hammond enjoyed the occasional choux bun, his enjoyment was purely in the consumption rather than the creation.

He sighed, his fingers hovering over the computer mouse. Was that the Audi he was looking for? He leaned closer to the screen, satisfied that the marks on the car were identical to the description he had been given. The image was not clear, but he logged it and printed what he could as a reference for the team debrief later that afternoon.

The sound of a banging door at the other end of the office interrupted his concentration and caused him to look up, seeking the source of the noise. The detectives standing by the water dispenser were engaged in conversation. Their heads were bent, eyes focused on the floor, their hands occasionally gesticulating. Hammond studied them, remembering that he had once been the same; a conscientious and purposeful detective. Investigations would often bring despair more than relief, but occasionally resulted in justice or, at the very least, a sense of closure. Where there were unanswered questions or lack of evidence to support the truth, though, the frustration and anguish were insurmountable.

Hammond had been a police officer for over 40 years, during which time he had witnessed every human condition imaginable, and that had meant sacrifices in his personal as well as his working life. He could never have been anything other than a police officer, but over the years the responsibility had weighed him down so much that he had felt ground down, gradually losing the energy or the drive to continue the relentless fight against law-breakers.

Crime solving was rarely black and white, good versus bad; over the years he had learnt that even the most decent, good-natured people could break the law, sometimes for their own survival. One year earlier, Hammond had aided in the arrest of a pensioner who had stabbed an armed burglar he had confronted in his home. The 78-year-old had been asleep with his wife when he heard noises, and was forced to retreat into his kitchen when he was confronted by one of the intruders who was armed with a screwdriver. Following a struggle in the kitchen, the burglar sustained a fatal stab wound to his chest. The scenario had felt unjust to everyone involved.

The wife, who had suffered from dementia and had, until that fateful night, been cared for by her husband, had been moved to social care where she died soon after. The aftermath had been widely reported in the media. Public opinion had been extreme, with confusion over which party was the victim. Some were in defence of the homeowner who had felt the need to protect himself and his wife, but many were angered by the violence used against the intruder.

It had been necessary to investigate with objectivity, but Hammond and his colleagues had struggled with their own consciences, and ultimately it was the jury that had decided to find the homeowner not guilty of murder with intent. But the damage had been done, and there were more victims than just the murdered man. The homeowner had gained a criminal record, lost his security and his wife, and it had been necessary for him to relocate due to threats against him from the intruder's friends and family.

If anyone had predicted how Hammond would spend his later life, he would have been aghast. Once he had been a fair-haired, idealistic young officer, happily married with a beautiful son, a lovely home, and the respect of his colleagues. Now he was no more than a grey-haired, divorced, lonely shell of a man, living in a cramped, dingy flat, enjoying the occasional visit from his son, but was disillusioned with his work, and ending his career amongst people he hardly knew.

Hammond had no expectation of anything else. He was resigned to fading out of his working life quietly and unnoticed, but still there was a glimmer of hope that something better was waiting for him following retirement. That there would be surprising and decisive events yet to happen.

His reverie was creating another headache, and he searched his wallet for the foil tray of paracetamol he now carried as a matter of course. Peering at computer screens didn't help. Eye strain was expected at his age, but the headaches were getting worse and occurring daily. He massaged the back of his neck whilst gathering the printed notes, then headed off to the debriefing room.

*

Hammond accepted his son's dinner invitation for the weekend with a mixture of pleasure and dread. Any opportunity to see Paul was always welcomed, but it was inevitable that Paul would be accompanied by his wife, Bettina – a woman whom Hammond despised. He did not consider himself to be a judgemental man, but in this instance, he was openly discriminate against the woman who had moulded his son into a replica of herself.

Bettina was the opposite of what a woman represented to Hammond. She had no grace, no respect or empathy for the less fortunate. As well as being – at 51 years of age – some 19 years Paul's senior, Bettina was a right-wing extremist, arrogant, and obstinate beyond reason. Neither did she possess any physical feminine attributes. It was a mystery what Paul had ever seen in the former tutor of Gender Studies, yet the pair had been married just over two years, and he had not given any impression of being anything other than content.

Hammond had replied to his son's emailed invitation as he was about to leave the office, but as he drove the short journey home, his mind was preoccupied with the thought of seeing Paul again and how he would be able to tolerate the presence of his daughter-in-law.

Hammond stopped at the traffic lights and watched a young woman crossing the road. She was not pretty, but attractive, casually dressed, with loose blonde hair resting on her shoulders. There was nothing remarkable about her, but Hammond appraised her as the kind of girl he would have wanted for Paul. You couldn't tell much about a person from seeing them cross the road, but she looked mild-mannered and amiable, and he imagined her having a name like Amelia.

Lost in his fantasy now, 'Amelia Hammond' sounded good. He would have toasted her at his son's wedding: 'To my new daughter, Amelia!' She would look good next to Lyn in the family photos, being of similar height and build. But he had only been told of his son's nuptials by text message and a link to a Facebook page. He hadn't been there to pin the corsage on his son's lapel, and had not been given the opportunity to shake his son's hand before the walk down the aisle. Instead, he had looked aghast at the images shared on social media of the frumpy, aging bride, dressed in a neutral trouser suit, looming over the slighter build of Paul.

The toot of a horn behind him alerted Hammond that the traffic lights had changed to green, and he raised a hand of apology in the rear-view mirror to the driver behind him, and accelerated right to Folkestone.

*

At 7am the following morning, Hammond arrived at the office with an almond croissant and a large Americano from Costa. It was a treat that needed to be savoured in peace and quiet. The office, with only the hypnotic hum of computers, was a viable environment for breakfast before it filled with the daily activity – unlike his flat, which was surrounded by the din of the latest construction projects. In preparation for Brexit, the roads were being widened, resurfaced, and remodelled. The prediction of a no-deal meant that the capacity for lorries travelling to Europe would be exhausted, hence the urgency for lorry parks to be provided around the South East. Consequently, £29million pounds paid by the taxpayer was rewarded with constant disruption to commuters and Kent residents.

The whole Brexit topic was shut away in the back of Hammond's mind. Like the majority of British voters, he was embarrassed by the political impasse. As he had waited in traffic on the way into work that morning, he listened to a news report that, in the early hours, EU leaders had agreed a 'Flextension' until Halloween, prolonging Britain's exit from the European Union even further.

Hammond had scoffed, imagining Bettina's reaction. He wondered if it was worth mentioning when he saw her that he had signed the petition to revoke Article 50 for a second referendum. There was no expectation that the petition would fulfil its objective, but just knowing he had signed it would make her hackles rise! He had enjoyed the fantasy of antagonising her so much that he had forgotten his usual annoyance at the congestion, and instead been content to sit grinning in the traffic queue.

The coffee was lukewarm but enjoyable whilst Hammond logged on to his emails. He was pleasantly surprised to see he had a message from Lois Dunn, now a Detective Inspector, having transferred to the Metropolitan Police one year previously. She had always been interested in climbing the ladder and had thoroughly deserved promotion. For several years, Dunn had worked under him as his Detective Sergeant and, despite their regular disagreements, they had worked as a good team.

Hammond was genuinely pleased she intended to attend his retirement party in a week's time. It would be good to catch up. He scanned his inbox, replying to the most urgent messages, whilst brushing croissant crumbs from the keyboard. The last mouthful had just been swallowed when the phone rang. It was Reception.

'We have someone here that needs to speak to someone regarding a missing person.'

'There are no officers downstairs that can deal with it?'

'I need supervisory oversight. The initial assessment indicated a possible risk.'

'I'll come down.'

Wallace replaced the phone and wondered aloud what he was doing. Missing people were not investigated by the Major Incident and Serious Crime Team, unless there was credible reason to suppose a crime had been committed. But he needed a project and, if all ended well, it would help to leave his career, believing he had achieved some success.

Within minutes, Hammond was seated next to a dark-haired woman in her early forties. She was well groomed and had taken time to look attractive, despite her obvious distress. She had introduced herself as Mischa Taylor, whose 54-year-old partner, Elijah Johnson, had not returned home since the previous evening.

Hammond glanced at the photograph Mischa had taken recently on her phone camera of the two of them posing in front of the London Eye. Elijah Johnson looked like a healthy, middle-aged man with a good head of greying hair, a wide nose, deep-set dark eyes, and a square jaw. He was of average height with a strong-looking physique. With no particularly distinguishing features, he could easily blend into a crowd without being noticed. The notes taken during the initial assessment stated there had been no contact from Elijah and no obvious reason for his absence, but Hammond wanted as much information as possible, and Mischa obliged, despite having to repeat what she had explained to the previous officer.

'On the days when I don't stay over, Elijah always phones me in the evening. Last night, when I hadn't heard from him, I called him. There was no answer. I tried about five or six times, and again this morning. It's not usual for him to ignore any missed calls. So, I went to his place this morning. I knew then he hadn't been home, because the dog had not been fed and the water bowl was almost empty. That's not normal. Elijah treats that dog as if it were his child.'

Hammond nodded reassuringly whilst scribbling notes. It was not essential to write down what she said, but he found it offered the impression of being proactive and gave the concerned party a sense that they were being taken seriously.

'When was the last time you spoke to Elijah?'

'Yesterday, around midday.'

'Did he say what his plans were for the remainder of the day?'

Mischa nodded. 'He was feeling positive. The weather was good in the morning, and he said he wanted to walk into Hythe town to the library.'

'Was this normal for Elijah?'

'Yes, he enjoys being outdoors and he goes to the library often. He likes to use the computer there.'

Hammond fixed his gaze on Mischa.

'You say Elijah was feeling positive. Would this suggest that some days he is not so positive? Does he struggle with negative emotions occasionally?'

Mischa paused. She seemed unsure how to answer, then she responded firmly, 'Elijah is not depressed. Occasionally he loses hope since he lost his job, but generally, he is emotionally stable and does not have financial worries. He has a steady income writing trivia quiz questions, but otherwise I earn enough for both of us.'

Suddenly Mischa leaned forward and looked at Hammond with an earnest expression.

'I know this suggests that Elijah has orchestrated his disappearance somehow, but you need to believe me, this is completely unlike him. That is why I am here. I *know* that something has gone terribly wrong. I've checked Accident and Emergency wards, tried his contacts, and his ex-wife. I've considered all the reasons why he has not returned home, and not one explains why he has not contacted me.'

Hammond approached his next question with care. 'Is there a chance that Elijah has kept anything from you?'

Mischa shook her head but did not respond.

'You told the Constable earlier that you and Elijah have been partners for one-and-a-half years. Can you describe your relationship with him?'

Mischa met Hammond's gaze as she responded. 'Both of us are divorcees; neither of us is interested in marriage, but our relationship is intimate and exclusive. We sleep together regularly but both of us enjoy our own company, so I don't stay overnight at his place often, nor he at mine. We trust and respect each other and we talk every day. I did consider the possibility that Elijah might have gone off with another woman or something like that, but even if he did, he would have arranged for Charlie to be fed. But that poor dog was dehydrated and hungry this morning, which Elijah would never allow.'

Hammond put his notes to the side and contemplated the woman beside him. He had seen false displays of anxiety many times, but Mischa was displaying utter confusion as well as distress, which convinced him she was genuine. He attempted to comfort her.

'It is less than twenty-four hours, so it is possible that Elijah has taken ill and was not able to contact you. However, I promise I will investigate all avenues of enquiry as a matter of priority, and we will stay in contact with you. Are there any dependants that need to be taken care of?'

Mischa shook her head. 'Just Charlie, his dog, but I'll keep him with me for the time being.' Her voice broke a little, hinting at the emotion that threatened to overwhelm her, but she regained her composure quickly. 'I won't go to work today, or at least until I have an idea what is happening.'

Hammond agreed to meet Mischa later that morning at Elijah's home, then he escorted her back to Reception before heading back upstairs to the office. He knocked at the door of Superintendent Brian Morris, who was struggling with a stuck drawer in the filing cabinet.

Quickly Hammond debriefed his commanding officer.

'The girlfriend said that Elijah has not been absent without notice before. I've done a run-down of his last known movements, but need to check with the library, cover his route to and from the town, and consider whether there were any diversions that his girlfriend was unaware of. There is an ex-wife, with whom I was told he shares an amiable relationship, so I will arrange to talk with her also.'

Morris nodded. 'Is there any chance that he had another woman on the side?'

Hammond shook his head. 'Nothing to suggest that, but we won't know for sure until we check his electronic communications or search his property. We've been given a list of his usual contacts, mainly from the town leisure club, such as his squash partners.'

Morris listened without speaking. His confidence in Hammond was evident. 'What is your feeling about this?'

Hammond inhaled deeply and considered his response before speaking. 'Personally, I agree there is a suggestion of risk. I don't want to wait and see what comes up. I would rather pursue any enquiries that I can. It doesn't seem as if Elijah just took some time out.'

'Although he is a divorcee who recently lost his job,' Morris pointed out. 'It could suggest he had reason to despair.'

Hammond smiled wryly. 'So says one divorcee to another!' He had meant it with light humour, but noticed Morris flinch slightly.

Then the senior officer smiled. 'Well, I guess in some cases divorce can be a cause for celebration. I guess we will know more once you've checked his personal effects.'

Hammond turned to leave but was called back.

'I can't offer resources at this point, so you are on your own for the time being. As soon as we know that there is a potential crime worth investigating, we'll reconsider the next course of action.'

Chapter Two

In an age where the majority of social interaction was effected through digital communication and 90 percent of the UK's population used the internet on a regular basis, Wallace Hammond was curious why Elijah Johnson regularly used a computer at a public library instead of using a personal computer within the private confines of his own home. He wondered whether an explanation would be offered during the search of Elijah's home and possessions, so headed there as his first point of call.

Elijah's home was a two-bedroom bungalow nestled in the middle of a quiet cul-de-sac, situated between the neighbouring towns of Hythe and New Romney. As Hammond approached, he could see Mischa waiting in a white Smart car parked on the kerb outside Elijah's front garden. He beckoned to her as he drew up along-side, but deliberately parked further along the road. It was better to conduct his initial search with discretion. No doubt the neighbours would be aware something was up before long.

Hammond strode up to the door where Mischa now stood, and accepted the keys from her hand.

'If I may, I'd look to take a quick look by myself, and then perhaps you can tell me if anything looks out of the ordinary.'

Mischa agreed to wait, and returned to her car where a Jack Russell terrier was yapping at the passenger window.

As Hammond entered the bungalow, he observed a winter coat hanging on the coat peg inside the entrance porch. He checked the pockets. A collection of unused dog waste disposal bags, a packet of travel tissues, and an opened tube of cough sweets were the only contents. A pair of rubber boots, size 9, were on the mat underneath. Hammond checked their soles; dry and relatively clean. He ventured through the interior porch door and paused between two doorways, one leading to the kitchen on his left.

Every time he entered another person's property, he had a guilty sense that he was trespassing, despite knowing it was a general practice in police work. Hammond had always felt uncomfortable with the task of searching through another's personal belongings. He shook the feeling off, telling himself he was not intruding but merely doing a preliminary check, and ventured further into the home.

The walls were painted off-white. The beige carpet lacked sufficient padded comfort underfoot. Wooden framed pictures of coastal landscapes and brightly coloured botanical prints decorated the walls in sporadic order. Hammond noted that not all were at eye level, causing him to stretch or bend to look at the images before he ran his hand gently at the back of each frame. They appeared to be reproduction prints by the same artist, signed with their initials in black on the bottom right of each picture. There was no other décor other than a yucca plant placed in a basket-style pot in the hallway.

The kitchen was small and basic, measuring about three by five metres, with a back door that led to the garden. Two usable sideboards ran along the opposing sides of the room. They were uncluttered but lacked workable space, partly due to the placement of a combination microwave, a twin toaster, and a kettle taking up most of the sideboard. Above them was a row of cupboards. Hammond checked in each one. The plates were mismatched – some plain, some with floral designs. He counted eight dinner plates and contemplated whether Elijah had enjoyed entertaining. Next, he checked the glassware; four wine glasses, the rest were tumblers. The washing machine had a few items awaiting a wash: socks, pants, jeans, and a few t-shirts. The oven seemed well used, the freezer well stocked. Under the sink were cleaning detergents and stacks of tinned dog food, a packet of canine flea treatment, and a small first aid kit.

A small square dining table, large enough for four places, was positioned by the window facing the road at the front. Hammond glanced at the pair of cork dinner mats – one was more worn than the other.

He re-entered the hallway to the living room, which was minimalistic but comfortable. A tan three-piece leather sofa was placed against the north wall, opposite a small television on a corner unit. There was a Panasonic old-style hi-fi supporting stacks of music cds, ranging from jazz, seventies to eighties pop classics, and soft rock. Hammond studied several books on the low bookshelf beside the window. The majority of titles were based on sport or sporting legends, but also wildlife photography, a complete works of Shakespeare, a biography of David Bowie, several art history books, a well-thumbed copy of the *Encyclopaedia Britannia*,

Whitaker's Almanac, *Kobbe's Complete Book of Opera*, Greek Mythology, and several titles based on British history.

Three framed photographs were displayed on the mantelpiece: a Jack Russell, presumably Charlie, running towards the photographer holding a tennis ball in its mouth; another of Mischa in a garden, smiling at the camera; the third showed Mischa and Elijah cuddled together, her head against his shoulder, looking directly at the camera. They looked happy.

He checked for any photo albums. Not finding any, he looked through the drawer of the corner unit. There was a packet of new AA batteries, television cables, and the television remote. Hammond looked for any signs of a computer. There were none, and no router. He checked the wall sockets. There was no landline connected to the phone socket. Evidently Elijah was modern enough to prefer a mobile phone, even if he did not have Wi-Fi.

The main bedroom next door was then examined. The bed had been used recently. Two empty suitcases were propped upright at the back of the built-in wardrobe, partially concealed by the ten shirts, varying in colours and patterns, a few jackets, several pairs of jeans, and formal plain trousers – all size 28 inch waist, ranging from navy to black. Several shoes, all in size 9, ranged from formal black leather to canvas summer plimsolls.

The first drawer of the chest of drawers contained a box of assorted cuff-links and a plain gold wedding ring. A valid passport was found on top of a small collection of birthday cards. Hammond flicked through the passport, taking a note of the number and expiry date before replacing and examining the greetings cards addressed to

Elijah which were piled underneath. Hammond opened them all, making a note of the names. A card with the picture of a Jack Russell sleeping was signed from Mischa with all her love; another, with photographs of sailing boats, had been signed 'Love Sue'. A crude cartoon of a buxom woman in tennis gear had been signed by several people. Hammond took a photo of the signatures and replaced the items in the drawer.

He checked the remaining contents – t-shirts and jumpers, underwear and socks, then ran his hand underneath each drawer base and peered behind the unit. There was nothing concealed.

Hammond surveyed the room carefully. The room had the basic essentials, but it lacked any hint of the personality of the individual who slept there. There may have been the intention to leave without a trace, or it could be indicative of a man who had yet to identify his own style.

Checking the spare room and bathroom, Hammond noted both toothbrushes in the cabinet and a comb, then checked the plughole in the bath and shower, and extracted hairs before putting them into an evidence bag. He repeated his inspection in each room, taking photographs using his mobile phone, then ventured into the back garden which consisted of a small patio, a square of lawn, and a washing line. He peered into the dustbins; they were full, suggesting constant usage. A quick examination of the lawn and patio showed no evidence of any disturbance in the ground.

Hammond identified the garage key from the fob Mischa had provided, and let himself in. The red Dacia Logan parked inside was clean, the doors locked. Hammond glanced in the windows. The car looked empty. The shelves on the far wall of the garage housed jars of screws and washers, the usual DIY equipment, and several Haynes Manuals. Hammond rifled through them, more out of self-interest than anything, and was bemused to find between the manuals for a Ford Escort and a Vauxhall Zafira that there was a Captain Scarlet Spectrum Agents Manual. He chuckled, resisting the temptation to read through it, and surveyed above him. Various lengths of rope, neatly wound and tied together, were stored beside a pile of folded plastic sheets on a board balancing between two rafters. A man's Apollo Enduro bike was hanging from the hooks screwed into the rafters.

Mischa smiled when he gestured to her from the door, inviting her to join him. As she opened the car door, Charlie came bounding up the short path.

'Poor boy, you miss your dad, eh?' Hammond attempted to pet the dog as it brushed past him, but Charlie continued to sniff the perimeter of each room, occasionally whining and looking up expectantly.

Mischa sighed in sympathy. She picked the dog up and cradled him in her arms before addressing Hammond. 'Did you find anything that could help?' Her tone suggested despondency.

Hammond inclined his head to the side in a gesture that was between a nod and a shake.

'It depends.' He said, 'Does Elijah have a computer? Is it likely he would have that with him?'

'I don't think he has the need for one of his own. The local library works for him as an office, because he can research there for the quiz questions he composes, and can use their printer. Otherwise, he uses his phone for emails or internet searches.'

Hammond accepted this explanation. He wasn't the most technically-minded of people himself. He sat down on the sofa and waited for Mischa to do the same.

'There doesn't seem to be much paraphernalia. There's not much here to give us an idea of what Elijah liked, or what kind of person he was.'

Mischa nodded. 'I agree. I used to think it was because he lived as a bachelor, but he had said the advantage of a divorce was that it taught you material objects were worthless in the greater scheme of things.' She raised a shoulder slightly, indicating she respected if not agreed with Elijah's thoughts.

'The divorce was amicable?' Hammond referred to her statement given during the preliminary interview.

'Yes, Elijah and Susan remain good friends. There was never any animosity between them, but I understood the relationship only lasted a few years from when they met to when they divorced. A whirlwind romance, I guess you would call it.'

Mischa leaned forward a little as if to confide a well-kept secret. 'Susan had money – her grandfather and father were entrepreneurs – and Elijah felt he didn't quite belong in her society. He was never comfortable with the pomp, as he called it. At least, that is the explanation he gave me.'

'Have you ever met Elijah's parents or any other members of his family?'

Mischa's expression was one of sympathy. 'No. He never mentioned family, other than his mother, whom I haven't met yet. He hasn't mentioned siblings or cousins, and there was never any mention of children that he knew or was close to. I assume he is an only child.'

Hammond nodded. 'So, what can you tell me about Elijah? Does he have any interests or hobbies? A Practising religion, that kind of thing?'

'He was not religious; at least, he was not involved with any church. He enjoyed sport. Watching sport as well as being active. In particular, playing squash at the Hythe Leisure Club. He liked doing anything outdoors, really.'

Hammond remembered the birthday card. 'Did Elijah sail at all?'

'No, not since I've known him.'

'Forgive me with the questions. I am sure it will be easy enough to look up, but if you don't mind telling me, is this bungalow a rented property?'

'No, Elijah owns it. He had just bought it before we met – early 2018, I think.'

'Thank you, like I say, it is easy enough to check, but no harm in asking.' Hammond offered a smile. He was aware that the questioning was sounding more like an interrogation, but there was a sense of unease he couldn't explain but did not want to show either.

'I assume Elijah carries a wallet with a driving licence and bank card with him, but his passport is here which suggests he has not gone abroad at least. Would you know where he keeps his bank statements or official documents?'

Mischa guided Hammond back to the main bedroom and lifted the bed mattress, revealing a linen drawer. Inside were neatly arranged folders containing bank statements, travel insurance confirmation letters, and numerous utility bills.

She offered a wry smile. 'He intended to buy a filing cabinet but hadn't got round to it. I expect there are more papers somewhere, but it's never been something I would have been interested in or have had a reason to discuss. We are financially independent of one another.' She paused for a second, glancing at the papers Hammond was shuffling through. 'It makes you realise how much you take for granted. I mean, I thought we were close, but only now I am realising I don't even know who he banks with.'

Hammond offered a reassuring smile. 'That's understandable. You are both independent, like you said, so there would be no reason to share every detail if you were happy just knowing the important bits.'

Mischa reluctantly accepted this logic and returned the smile. 'I guess so. I have always liked my own space and I know he was similar that way.' She shrugged and looked past Hammond as Charlie started circling on the floor. 'Excuse me. I think I need to take Charlie into the garden.' She whistled for the dog to follow her, leaving Hammond alone in the bedroom.

He scanned the room again with his eyes and tried to imagine Elijah at home alone. What were his habits? The house was tidy and comfortable, but the atmosphere was practical rather than homely. Perhaps that was just a simplistic way of living?

Hammond considered his own lodgings. What did his apartment tell anyone walking in? That he was disorganised, unsettled maybe. Ever since he had moved into his Folkestone apartment, he had never considered it to be anything other than a convenient stop-over. Maybe it was the same with Elijah. Hammond sighed. He had always considered his home as being the house in Stansted which he had shared with Lyn and Paul, but now Lyn had remarried and Paul was grown up. Maybe he would never again enjoy the sense of having a real home. Hammond wondered if Elijah felt the same.

He heard Mischa approach from the hallway and smiled as he met her at the bedroom door.

'I think that's it for now,' he said, 'unless you have found anything to be missing or out of place?'

Mischa shook her head. 'No, it all looks pretty normal. Thank you for checking.'

She hesitated, placing her hand on Hammond's arm for emphasis as she continued, 'I'm sorry, it must seem as if I am making a big fuss over nothing, but you know when you just have this feeling that something isn't right? I've got that feeling. I don't know what could possibly be wrong, but I have this urge to find him quickly, I'm actually feeling a bit scared!' She ended her sentence with a short laugh, as if aware that she was coming across as dramatic, but her utterance was devoid of humour.

Hammond followed Mischa back to the porch. Trying to be as reassuring as possible, he promised to update her on any news as he handed back the door keys. Then he stopped, instinctively looking up at the loft door above him in the hallway. For a moment he considered checking the roof space, but reminded himself there was no need to be so thorough at this stage.

They didn't know what they were looking for at this time, or even if Elijah's absence was a cause for concern.

Hammond waited whilst Mischa locked the door behind them then walked her to her car. He waved her off until her car disappeared around the corner, resisting the temptation to wave at the neighbour who was watching him through her net curtains, and headed back to his car.

As Hammond exited the cul-de-sac onto the main road, he considered his next port of call. There was nothing to suggest any foul play in Elijah's disappearance, so he wouldn't be justified spending more time searching. He deliberated whether it would make more sense to call in at the library. Elijah's last known movements could be traced before Hammond drove the further five miles to where the ex-wife lived, but he concluded it was more likely Elijah's friends and family would know if there was any real cause for concern. Evidently, Mischa was genuinely worried, but there could be a simple explanation for Elijah's lack of contact. Maybe Elijah was not as open about his life as she believed him to be.

As Hammond followed the directions towards the home of Susan Maxwell, he hoped that there *was* a simple explanation, if only to ease the niggle he had in the pit of stomach that Mischa's instinct was right and Elijah Johnson was in genuine trouble.

CHAPTER THREE

The rain was falling as sheets of water cascading over the two men as they disembarked the bus. Much as Elijah wanted to, he could not leave the other man, since their wrists had been bound together with the plant tie that had been attached before he had realised what was happening. Elijah felt sick; he had no idea what was happening.

The panic was creating a nervous energy that one minute froze his reactions, the next propelled his body to move automatically. He part-stumbled, part-jogged beside his companion as they crossed the road towards the main canal path. Nobody looked at them. The pedestrians around them were covering their heads with hoods or bags as they rushed to find shelter from the rain.

'Pull your jacket over your head,' he was instructed, and blindly obeyed.

They hurried over the narrow footbridge, Elijah half dragged by the man whose pace exceeded his own.

'Where are you taking me?'

Elijah was bewildered. The man was taking him towards the main road. He looked towards the vans that were parked along the pavement, expecting side doors to suddenly open and arms to grab him. This was a serious situation; he knew it, and he was genuinely scared.

To his surprise, they did not go alongside the vans, but instead he was pushed down the canal bank, his feet sliding underneath him on the mud, the undergrowth scratching his face. He gasped as the air was knocked out of his lungs, and he wondered if he was about to be pushed into the water. The man was going to drown him.

Please no!' he whimpered.

But his companion was pulling him up. Elijah's knee dragged in the mud as his other leg struggled to straighten. Eventually, his foot found enough grip in the undergrowth and he managed to stand and stumble as they headed towards a small stone shelter hidden in the canal bank. It was incredible. All these years Elijah had lived a few miles away, had walked this route hundreds of times, but had never noticed this place before.

He thought they were seeking shelter from the rain and tried to take in a breath, but instead he was pulled onwards. They stumbled over debris and broken stone further into the depths. It was pitch black and the smell was putrid, the air around them heavy and clammy.

Suddenly, his companion stopped and pushed Elijah against a wall. He felt something cold and sharp against his wrist and inhaled sharply, his lungs resisting the impure intake of stale, damp air, which caused him to cough. The sudden choking rocked his upper body forwards.

'Stand still. Don't move,' he was instructed, as he felt the tension around his wrist suddenly release.

There was the sound of stones being turned, clattering and thuds, and then a firm hand on his shoulder half-pulled, half-pushed him. Another hand pushed his head down towards his chest.

'Bend as you move forward,' he was told.

He did so, but tottered over lumps of solid debris underfoot. Then suddenly his feet found softer ground. In a moment of clear thinking, he managed to extract his phone from his pocket and threw it behind him, just before he felt the other man's body press close against his for several seconds. Then he was pushed forwards. 'Keep moving!'

Elijah followed the instructions, not knowing what else he could do. His heartbeat was thumping in his ears, the panic making him feel sick as he advanced further into total darkness.

CHAPTER FOUR

As Hammond turned into the drive towards Susan Maxwell's house, he wished he had adopted his late father's habit of always carrying a comb in his jacket pocket. Wealthy people who lived in large homes had always intimidated Hammond, which he knew was completely irrational, but he felt inadequate whenever he was confronted by any display of opulence.

He parked the car in the corner furthest away from the house then walked towards the porch, conscious that the doorbell was the kind that had a camera on it, and that someone was watching him. The door opened within minutes and a petite, very slender lady, with light grey hair pulled back from her face, beamed at him with such a welcoming manner that Hammond incorrectly presumed she was expecting a friend at the door instead of a stranger.

They shook hands as she introduced herself as Susan, Elijah's ex-wife. Hammond explained the reason for his visit, and she nodded slowly as he spoke. She didn't invite him inside the house, but remained in the porch, leaning against the door frame as they conversed.

'Mischa phoned earlier this morning with the same enquiry. I confess, I don't think I can be of any help. I haven't seen Elijah for a while now.'

'But you are still in contact?' Hammond asked.

Susan nodded. 'Yes, we are friendly, but we don't socialise in the same circles, so I don't see him that often.'

As Hammond went to continue with his questioning, she suddenly interrupted, 'I'm not too worried, though. Elijah is his own man, always has been. As I have said to Mischa, it's possible that he just had a flight of fancy to go off somewhere and simply hasn't thought to read his texts, or maybe his phone needs charging. I'm sure that this mystery will soon be resolved.' She ended the sentence with a slight lilt, giving the expression of a lack of concern, but it was obvious Susan had no intention of prolonging the conversation.

'Do you have any idea where he would go if he wanted to be alone? Or any such reason for wanting to?'

She shook her head. 'I've no idea. We used to be married, but that doesn't mean I keep tabs on him! He's a grown man, and I am sure he is capable of taking care of himself!' Her tone had changed; she was almost sounding haughty.

Hammond realised he would not make any progress with his line of questioning. There was nothing more he could do, so he thanked her and returned to Folkestone. He drove slowly, his thoughts preoccupied. His headache was coming back.

*

On Friday morning, Hammond awoke with a blinding headache. He phoned the office and told them he was taking the day off sick. It was unusual for him to admit defeat so easily to a physical ailment, but he was too exhausted to move out the bed.

'I'll be ok after a good sleep,' he said to Superintendent Morris, after he had apologised.

'It's probably your blood pressure,' Morris suggested rather unhelpfully. 'You should get it checked.'

Hammond didn't reply.

'I've read the report you left yesterday,' Morris went on. 'There is not enough evidence to suggest an investigation is warranted. To be fair, we responded quite beyond the norm already, since he hadn't been missing that long. I've referred it to Missing Persons. Hopefully, Mr Johnson will pop up in the meantime, but if he doesn't, it is more their domain than ours.'

Hammond mumbled a reply; his head felt as if it was about to burst. Morris took the hint and ended the call.

Hammond slept for several hours. When he awoke, it was late afternoon. His head and neck were tender and he was nauseous, but managed to consume some soup and swallow some painkillers without gagging. By evening, he felt well enough to get out of bed again and walk around his apartment. He felt stiff, and had to bend his body in several positions to flex the muscles.

I'm old, he thought. *I'm creaking like an old ship.*

He sat on the toilet longer than he needed to, his mind drifting from one thought to another. He studied the grouting around the bathroom tiles and noticed flecks of black mould were starting to appear and the bathroom lino was worn around the bath. He found himself looking up at the ceiling and questioning why he had moved into an apartment he had no appreciation for.

His observations were of no use to him at that time, but he hadn't the energy to stand up after he had finished his business. Eventually, he decided he may as well go back to his bed, where he slept heavily for another twelve hours.

*

Hammond was wakened in the early hours by a dog barking; He lay in bed for a while, plumping his pillow around his ears to dampen the sound, but by the third attempt he was awake. He sat up slowly and waited for his head to protest, but was relieved to discover the headache had eased. He considered whether he should eat something and was encouraged that the thought didn't sicken him, so he shuffled into the kitchen and toasted the last few slices of bread from the back of the top cupboard, remembering too late he had used up the last of the Marmite two days before.

He groaned inwardly, remembering he had meant to go grocery shopping the previous evening. Paul was expected that evening and he had no dinner to offer. Ordering a take-away would be insufficient; he wanted to cook for his son, since he hadn't seen him for a while. But it was his day off, so shopping for his son would be his priority.

The teabag had torn but Hammond used it anyway, ignoring the occasional wash of grit as he downed his tea and munched on toast whilst reading the news headlines from his phone. He deliberately ignored the updates on Brexit, but found himself uttering the occasional swear word when he read about President Trump's latest *faux pas*.

The local news didn't offer anything more enlightening; more road works and long delays were expected as the new smart motorways were being installed. The scheme to increase capacity whilst minimising environmental impact and reducing congestion was, in his opinion, a money-saving scheme that was, in reality, a death trap for stranded motorists. His cynicism was exclaimed out loud, despite having no-one there to hear him. He scanned the rest of the local headlines looking for any reports on Elijah Johnson's disappearance then, not finding any, abandoned the news entirely and considered the time.

The supermarket wouldn't open for another two hours. He showered and dressed before stripping the bed sheets, selecting the hot wash, then leaving the washing machine to do its job.

It was 6am, the sun was already shining bright, and there wasn't a cloud in the sky. As Hammond walked to his car, he listened to the halyards slapping against the masts of the boats in the harbour, the seagulls crooning. The early morning symphony was a welcome introduction to the day. Hammond breathed in the cool fresh air and decided that such a day was to be enjoyed. He was not going to waste time worrying or thinking negatively. It was going to be a good day.

It had been a random decision to continue onto the motorway towards Dover, but Hammond thought it would be nice to indulge in a coastal walk whilst he waited for the supermarket to open. The driver's window was open, and he enjoyed feeling the breeze against his face as he listened to the radio and enjoyed the time to himself. The car continued past Dover, taking him beyond the cliffs towards Deal. Country roads curved, and he enjoyed the swaying motion as the car glided along; machine and man in harmony on the open road.

On impulse, he took a side road leading towards a church, where he parked the car and wandered through the church yard, suddenly wishing he had a dog to accompany him. He found himself wondering again what he would do after he was retired from police work; he had no idea how to occupy himself, but maybe a dog would help him to get out and enjoy the country air more.

As he wandered aimlessly, he found himself heading towards a row of houses, where a *For Sale* sign was swinging by its hinges in the breeze. He stood before the period building for a while, considering the potential, aware of a bubble of excitement rising in his chest. Could he see himself living here? The property wasn't secluded, so it wasn't his dream home, but it was attractive and the road in which it was positioned was quiet. The house had evidently been modernised over the years, but he admired the chimney and imagined the original fireplace inside. He stood for several minutes considering the possibilities before thinking he might look suspicious gazing up at the window of a strange house, so he noted the estate agent's details and walked back to his car. He hadn't planned on moving home, but now the seed of thought had been planted in his brain he found himself becoming excited at the thought of starting a new life.

Yes, he thought. *I'll retire graciously; I will move to a cottage in the country and get a dog. My days will be spent walking and absorbing the joys of nature, and seeing life the way it was meant to be.* Too much time had been spent investigating how other people's lives had been shattered by one means or another, but now it was time to see how life could be wholesome.

*

Four hours later, Hammond was seated at his kitchen table examining property prospectuses and floorplans, considering a new life, when the apartment buzzer alerted an arrival. He was surprised to see Paul outside his door, much earlier than expected. Automatically his eyes looked beyond Paul into the corridor, his reservation at seeing Bettina all too evident.

Paul sighed as he ventured through the door. 'It's ok. I'm alone.'

He slapped his father on the shoulder as a token of affection. 'I know I'm early, but I figured we could spend some time together. I know it's your day off.'

Hammond took Paul to the kitchen where he busied himself filling the kettle, getting cups out of the cupboard, and retrieving the packet of chocolate digestives purchased that morning.

Behind him, Paul had seen the paperwork on the table. 'You're thinking of moving?'

'Yes, I figured it is time for a change of scenery.'

'It's a good idea. You need to do something with your life before it's too late.'

Hammond turned abruptly, setting the cups down on the worktop with more force than he intended. He found Paul's implication offensive. 'What's that supposed to mean?'

'Sorry, Dad, I didn't mean to offend you. I'm just a bit tetchy.' Paul offered a weak smile and sat himself at the table.

As Hammond set the hot drinks on the table, he noticed that Paul was sitting in the same way he did when he was tired or upset as a young boy.

'Do you want to talk about it?' he offered.

Paul shook his head then hesitated. 'Maybe. I don't know, there's not much to talk about.'

'But something is bothering you?'

Paul nodded, but then shrugged and turned his attention to outside the window at the street below. 'Forget it,' he said. 'It's nothing.'

*

The indigestion was more than uncomfortable, it was becoming embarrassing. Hammond had the need to expel gas but was unable to do it privately, and it was becoming increasingly difficult to hold in. He should have refused the offer of a kebab the previous evening and insisted on cooking for Paul, as he had originally intended, but the five-mile afternoon walk together to the pub had been pleasant, even if it had induced a ravenous appetite that had resulted in him bingeing on food his stomach couldn't digest.

Hammond quickly excused himself and had just made it to the corridor before the fart escaped. He furtively looked up the hallway, hoping no-one had heard him, before re-entering the office where DS Tom Edwards was waiting to resume their conversation.

'I did explain that search teams were on standby and the Missing Persons' Team was following any leads, but she insisted on talking to you.' Edwards sat with his back to the window, causing his greying hair to glisten as a white halo.

Hammond raised his eyebrows. 'But Mischa didn't give any indication as to what she wanted to talk about?'

Edwards shook his head. 'No, she was evasive. I didn't press her for any information.' He passed the scrawled message to Hammond with Mischa Taylor's phone number.

'Fine, I'll see her, but don't tell Morris yet. He doesn't want our time spent on this, as it isn't really our responsibility.' Hammond stopped speaking, realising that Edwards was more interested in looking at his phone, which had been beeping constantly since his arrival at the station that morning.

'Is everything ok?' he asked Edwards.

His colleague nodded distractedly. Then he looked up at Hammond, his face reddening with an expression of embarrassment or anger; Hammond couldn't tell which.

'Mind if I tag along? I could do with the distraction,' Edwards said.

Hammond drove westwards towards Mischa's preferred meeting place. It was a seven-mile journey, most of which was spent in silence. It was evident Edwards was lost in thought, but Hammond had no wish to press him. It seemed he wasn't the most trusted of counsels, if both Paul and Edwards didn't have the confidence to share their troubles with him.

Mischa was waiting in the coffee shop along the main road. She waved from the window as Hammond crossed the road towards her, but frowned when she saw he had company.

'It's ok,' Hammond told her as he sat down opposite her, 'DS Edwards is one of my most trusted colleagues, as well as my good friend.' Edwards looked almost sheepish at the glowing introduction as he shook her hand across the table.

Mischa hesitated, her complexion reddening as she plunged into a confession.

'I haven't been entirely straight with you.' She shifted in her seat a little before taking a sip of her drink and resuming, 'When I told you that I thought Elijah was in trouble, I really believed it. I still don't know what exactly, but there's this…' She passed an envelope across the table towards Hammond.

Inside were several printed emails addressed to Elijah. The messages were short, and written in capital fonts.

YOU ARE TO PAY FOR WHAT YOU HAVE DONE. BE WARNED.

Hammond raised an eyebrow and passed the first one to Edwards then shuffled through the next. There were about eight in total, all addressed to Elijah's email account from the same sender: thewronged@gmail.com.

YOU DESERVE TO SUFFER THE WAY YOU HAVE MADE US SUFFER.

The content of the messages differed slightly but the threats continued, apportioning blame on Elijah for something unmentioned.

Mischa waited for Hammond to say something, but instead he allowed her the opportunity to speak whilst he noted the times and dates of the messages.

'I didn't want to admit to you that I had gone into Elijah's email account without his permission.' Mischa flushed. 'I only did it because I was worried, then I saw these… that is why I have been so frightened. I couldn't tell anyone that I had read them, because I thought I would be in trouble for hacking into a private account. But when the enquiries were taken over by Missing Persons, I thought it wouldn't be taken seriously unless I shared these with you.' Mischa's voice cracked.

Hammond sympathised. She had good reason to be distressed.

'You've done the right thing showing us,' he reassured her. 'You won't get into trouble, but I agree this needs to be taken very seriously. We need to trace the sender of these messages. Do you have any idea what they are referring to?'

Mischa shook her head. 'I have absolutely no idea. I can't believe that Elijah has behaved in a vindictive way or done anything harmful to anyone. He's just not the type.'

Edwards spoke up. 'These have been sent over the course of three months. The last one was dated 25th March, that's two weeks ago. Elijah's been missing four days now. Have there been any messages sent to his account during the last four or five days?'

Mischa shook her head. 'No, I checked again this morning.'

Hammond leaned forward so that his full attention was on Mischa. 'Is there anything else you haven't told me?'

Mischa's reply was firm. 'No.'

Hammond nodded; he trusted she was being honest. He gathered all the messages and returned them to the envelope.

'I need to take these with me. But from now on, we will be looking into Elijah's disappearance,' he told her. 'I agree it looks likely that he is a deliberate target with someone with a vendetta.'

CHAPTER FIVE

At five minutes past nine on Monday morning, Hammond left the debriefing room with a throbbing headache and a craving for strong coffee. He had spent most of the previous night talking to Paul about everything except the reason Paul had chosen to sleep at his father's apartment for the last two nights instead of returning home to his wife.

Hammond hadn't questioned his son; it was none of his business unless Paul chose to confide in him, but it was evident Paul was going through some inner turmoil. Whilst he hated the idea of his son being miserable, he secretly hoped that Paul had seen sense and was questioning his marriage. It was no secret that Hammond could not tolerate Paul's wife Bettina. He wanted his son to be happy, and Hammond had no confidence that Bettina was capable of considering anyone's wellbeing beyond her own political ideals.

The debriefing this morning had not been long. Hammond had only two other officers helping him investigate the disappearance of Elijah Jonson. He would have preferred more manpower, but expected to be told that resources couldn't be spared. DS Tom Edwards had been delegated as his second-in-command, which would normally have been reassuring, but at the moment he seemed too distracted to be much help. When he wasn't interrupted by the constant beeping of incoming texts on his phone, his mind was elsewhere. Hammond was tempted to suggest Edwards take leave for a few days. There was no point in him being here if he couldn't focus on the job.

As if aware he was the subject of Hammond's thoughts, Edwards looked up as he approached.

'There's still no signal from Johnson's phone, but I've left DS Williams to request for the tech team to look into his email messages,' he said. 'It may be possible to trace the sender. If he has got any threats sent to his phone, that would take longer to find, but maybe he received something in the post?'

Hammond shook his head. 'There was no post when I searched the property, and as far as I know Mischa hadn't collected any. I guess it won't hurt to look again, though. I'm heading to Hythe library, so I can check the house again after that. Are you coming?'

It would be good to have a fresh pair of eyes looking at the house, but the car journey would also give Hammond a chance to talk to Edwards privately.

*

'You owe me an explanation.' Hammond returned to the car with two paper cups of petrol station coffee. It was weak but it would have to suffice. He slurped some of the liquid quickly before replacing the cap and handing the cup for Edwards to hold whilst he exited the forecourt and rejoined the A20.

Edwards shifted his weight in the passenger seat, awkwardly holding his arms out above the footwell in case the hot drinks spilled onto his lap.

'Not sure what explanation I owe you.' Edwards turned towards Hammond, his eyebrows raised.

Hammond sighed. 'Obviously there is something on your mind. I respect your privacy, but if we are to work together, I need to know you are willing to share your attention. If not, then you need to sort out whatever it is that's holding you back and return to work when the situation is resolved.'

Edwards blustered. 'Of course, you're never pre-occupied, are you?' His tone was sarcastic, but his comment was fair.

It was true that Hammond was often distracted. Only this morning, his mind had been on Paul whilst Superintendent Morris was being updated on the emails Mischa had uncovered.

'Fair enough,' he admitted, 'but if you need time off to be with the family or whatever, just take it.'

Edwards sighed, a long drawn out escape of air that spoke of his despondency. 'To be honest, I think it's best I stay out of the family's way right now. I need to be working, Wallace. But I'm sorry I have been distracted. From now on I'll be more focused.'

Hammonds shot him a sideways glance. 'I'd like to help you if I can. You can talk to me anytime. I'd like to think we are friends as well as colleagues.'

Edwards nodded silently and the car wound down the long hill towards Hythe.

*

Amongst the muted colours of light wooden book-shelves, cream walls and beige carpets, the blonde lady with her cobalt blue skirt and orange jumper stood out like a welcoming beacon of hope as Hammond entered the library. She was in her late thirties or early forties, her manner amiable, but her body language suggested she was self-conscious, almost shy. She looked up and smiled as Hammond approached the desk, and moved to the furthest end of the counter when he showed her his Police Identification.

Hammond returned the smile, appreciating the consideration she had shown to prevent customers overhearing their conversation as he introduced himself and Edwards. He noted she flushed a deep pink when he mentioned Elijah Johnson's name. The librarian's badge identified her as Alice.

'I was aware that the Police had been here the other day asking about Mr Johnson, but we were not given any explanation. Is he ok?' Alice's tone had risen slightly, indicating a genuine concern.

'That is what we need to ascertain.' Hammond spoke with a reassuring tone. 'From what we understand, Mr Johnson was here last Wednesday, but he hasn't been seen since.'

She nodded. 'Yes, he was here from late afternoon until we closed just after six in the evening.'

'Did he say where he was heading next?'

'No.'

'I understand that Mr Johnson is a regular visitor here. Does he use the computers?'

Alice nodded. 'Yes, normally he comes here about three or four days a week. He doesn't always use the computer, but I normally reserve him an hour's slot just in case.'

Hammond nodded absent-mindedly whilst he surveyed the row of five computers lined up opposite the desk.

'Is there a particular computer Mr Johnson favours?'

Alice gestured upstairs to the mezzanine above the counter. 'There is a computer upstairs that I think he prefers to use. He normally works at the same place at the desk up there.'

Edwards followed the stairs up to the mezzanine. After a few minutes he leaned over the banister and caught Hammond's eye, twisting his mouth slightly as if to communicate he had not discovered anything of interest.

Hammond paused his questioning whilst Alice served a customer. He watched her with interest, noting how she had predicted her customer's requirements before they had even asked. She had logged onto their accounts and gathered the information they required within seconds of their enquiry. The woman was efficient; if there was any information to be gathered on Elijah's particular habits or routine, it was likely Alice would provide it.

'Forgive the questions, but we are as yet none the wiser about the reason behind Mr Johnson's disappearance. If he is a regular here, I presume that you are familiar with his routine, or occasionally have the opportunity to talk to him? Is there anything that seemed to be out of the ordinary recently?'

Alice frowned as she considered the question. 'No, I don't think so. We did talk occasionally, but it was more a polite chat about the weather or whatever. There were days when he seemed quieter than usual, but I presume that was because he was concentrating on his research.'

Edwards had returned downstairs and stood, leaning slightly against the counter. 'Does Mr Johnson ever take any books home with him, or is he a customer that comes here mainly to use the space and facilities?' he asked.

Alice looked at Edwards with a quizzical expression. 'He has borrowed books in the past, or sometimes a DVD or music CDs, but mainly he uses titles that can't be taken home, such as local history directories or he uses the computer.'

Edwards looked at Hammond and raised his eyebrows. Hammond nodded, understanding what Edwards was communicating.

'We may need to look at the computer that Mr Johnson used,' he told the librarian. 'Is there a way you could track his usage?'

Alice nodded hesitantly. 'Yes, every customer has their own unique account and login, but you won't be able to check his account history without permission. I won't be authorised to allow you to look now or be able to look myself. We have to request the I.T. department to do that. You will have to contact my supervisor directly.'

Hammond took the details she had written down for him then smiled at Alice and thanked her for her cooperation. As he did so, he noted how thin wisps of hair had worked themselves loose from her chignon and framed her face so delicately it reminded him of Raffaello's Angeli Cherubini painting.

*

'If he had left the library and headed home, which direction is he likely to have headed?'

Edwards and Hammond paused outside the library, considering their next move. In front of the library car park was a green area that led to the canal path, beside them was a children's play area, and to their left was the road exit that took them towards the high street.

'We know he didn't take the car, which means he either walked home along the canal path heading west or he intended to get a bus from town.'

Edwards pointed at the council offices next door to the library building. 'Their CCTV cameras are pointed three ways, so there is bound to be some footage of Elijah leaving and heading in any of those directions.'

Hammond left Edwards to check at the council offices whilst he walked around and checked with the pharmacy and doctor's surgery around the corner. Within minutes they had submitted their requests for camera surveillance covering all directions.

Hammond felt despondent. 'I feel like we are getting nowhere,' he complained to Edwards as they returned to the car. 'Elijah has been missing for four days. We need to act fast, but instead it feels like we are losing valuable time just wandering from one place to the next. We need to make a public appeal.'

Edwards phoned the station and gave instruction to DS Williams to release a media statement. As he was occupied, Hammond turned the car towards the nearest bus stop and parked on yellow lines nearby, then sprinted over to the next bus that stopped. He boarded the bus and spoke to the driver, handed him a recent copy of Elijah's description, then returned to the car.

'Right, so now we should have enough surveillance to wade through for last Wednesday evening. If we assume that Elijah decided to travel by bus home, there are three possible buses he may have taken – the earliest was at 18.23; then another at 18.53; and another half an hour later. So, if he left the library just after 6, he had about twenty minutes before the next bus. What was the weather like then?' Hammond turned to Edwards. 'Can you remember?'

Edwards nodded. 'It rained heavily from about half past six.'

Hammond sighed. 'Then we will have to presume he took the first bus.' He paused. 'The shelters aren't entirely weather-proof, so he would have either waited and got drenched or possibly killed time over there...' Hammond pointed at the small supermarket opposite the bus stop. 'I'll go and check.'

*

Hammond and Edwards drove to Elijah Johnson's home with renewed hope. They now knew that he had boarded the 102 bus just after twenty minutes past six after purchasing a few groceries at the supermarket opposite, and had been identified by the cashier as a regular customer. CCTV from the bus had also been requested.

Hammond parked outside Elijah's bungalow and was immediately aware that the neighbour had noticed their arrival. He saw the curtain twitch several times. As he exited the car, he waved at the window. The curtains stopped moving.

It was evident that Mischa had visited the house since Hammond had last been there, as the bins had been moved to the front of the drive. Hammond looked inside and was disappointed to see that the recyclable waste had been collected. If there had been a threatening letter sent in the post, it was likely Elijah would have disposed of it, but now they would not know. Hammond sighed, then wandered around to the back of the house and found the key where Mischa had left it for him. They let themselves in the back door and entered the kitchen.

'So, what are we looking for exactly?' Edwards surveyed the room.

Hammond shrugged. 'Anything that may seem unusual. I've looked already, but it was more of a casual rummage. If we look together, we may just find something.'

Edwards exhaled slowly and concentrated on wandering around the room, looking in drawers and cupboards. Then he got down on all fours, examining the surface of skirting boards and the exposed sides of the kitchen units.

'There are no signs of disturbance, but this hasn't been scrubbed clean recently either, so I guess that suggests that there has been no attempt to cover up any crime scene.' Edwards stood up and ventured into the hallway.

He repeated the motions of Hammond's earlier search, checking the coats and shoes in the hallway, then examined the lock and the seal of the front door. 'No sign of an attempted break-in,' he called to his colleague.

Hammond stood inside the hallway watching Edwards. There had been many times when he had entered a property for a second time and had known whether someone else had been there in the interim. He couldn't explain the feeling that he had, but in most cases, he had been proved right. Now, as he stood in the hallway, he had that feeling again. As if he could see in his mind's eye a figure searching the house.

He looked around him, trying to see what anyone would have looked for, and then, almost instinctively, he looked up.

Something was different. He stood there, the feeling of unease growing. He was seeing something, without registering what. Edwards was moving around the house, muttering his observations but Hammond wasn't listening. He remained standing in the same spot, looking up. Then he walked back a few paces towards the kitchen door and looked back at the spot. Then he walked towards the living room and looked back.

And then he saw it.

The direction of light from the hallway was catching something glinting by the loft hatch. The loft door had been opened, but the latch hadn't fully engaged.

'Edwards!' Hammond's voice alerted his colleague who came immediately, looking up at where Hammond's attention was directed.

'This has been opened since I last came,' Hammond said.

Edwards took a chair from the kitchen and dragged it to underneath the loft hatch. 'Give me a leg up,' he said, then pushed the loft door open with his hand until it slammed back.

Hammond hoisted his colleague until Edwards' upper arms were resting on the timber frame inside the aperture. After a few grunts, Edwards managed to wriggle himself into the loft. A few seconds later, a light glowed from the darkness above.

'You coming up?' Edwards lay on his stomach and offered an arm to help him up. Hammond snorted; he might not be as heavy as he once was, but he had no confidence that he or Edwards were fit enough to survive the attempt, so he ventured out to the garden for something he could use as a ladder. The garage was locked, and there was nothing that could help.

Admitting defeat, he returned to the hallway and shouted up to Edwards, 'Is there anything?'

There was the sound of shuffling on boards then Edwards spoke. 'A few boxes. It's hard to tell if anything is missing, but...' There was a flash of light then Edwards appeared at the hatch opening, looking down at Hammond. He lowered his mobile phone towards him.

At first, Hammond couldn't see what Edwards was showing him. He peered closer to the photograph on the screen. Then he noticed a red smear on the wood timbers.

'Blood?'

'Well, if it is, it's not that old,' Edwards replied. 'It is still an almost red colour, but it's definitely not varnish, nor paint. If this is blood, there are a few droplets leading to or from a nail on one of the timbers by the door.'

Hammond considered for a few seconds, then said, 'Is there anything to suggest that something has been removed or added recently?'

There was silence from above him then Edwards appeared at the opening again. He sat on the edge and slowly lowered his legs towards Hammond, who took his weight and lowered his colleague to the chair. Edwards was dusty, and he coughed as he brushed installation foam residue off his clothes, then returned the chair to its original place in the kitchen.

'There are a few boxes, about four,' he explained. 'Most contained photograph albums, but there was one that had possibly been opened recently.'

Edwards directed Hammond's attention to another photograph that he taken on his mobile phone. Most of the boxes had been sealed in a similar way: one side flap had been folded above the larger flap, and the other side had been folded underneath the larger flap, so that the box had been closed without the use of tape.

But one box had all sides pressed closed by being wedged in between two other boxes.

'What was in this box?' Hammond asked.

'Papers mainly. Most referred to travel itineraries, The Panorama Hotel accommodation in Zagreb, and the European Quizzing Championship itinerary for 2017.'

'Nothing else?'

'No, just itineraries, information booklets on the competitors, that kind of thing.'

Hammond thought for a while and then he remembered. He went into the main bedroom and opened the linen drawer under the bed mattress. The papers were as he had left them, and he selected the pages he had remembered seeing. Travel insurance for Croatia, November 2017.

He looked at Edwards. 'I don't know what I'm thinking, but I want to take a note of these. I'm going to ask Morris if we can get a team to look in the loft, to take a note of the box contents and maybe check that it is blood on the timbers.' He was pondering aloud, but Edwards considered the words seriously.

'I can't see Morris agreeing,' he replied. 'It's a waste of resources; there's no body, no evidence of a crime. If that is blood, it could be the girlfriend's, or even Elijah's. It's not enough to justify money spent on a possible.'

Hammond agreed with a sigh. 'Ok, but make sure you send a copy of the photographs you took today so that we have it on record.'

They replaced the travel insurance papers where they had left them and walked to the back door. As they locked the back door and returned the key to its hiding place underneath a loose paving slab, Hammond was aware that he was being watched. He looked up, acknowledging the elderly lady who was peering at him over the neighbouring fence.

'Hello.' He greeted her with a smile and automatically produced his Police Identification. The woman didn't reply, but peered closer at his card and sniffed with indignation. Then she eyed him suspiciously.

'Is he Police as well?' She pointed with an arthritically stiff finger at Edwards, who reappeared by the garden gate. Hammond introduced his colleague with a friendly manner.

'So, what's he done then?'

'Are you referring to Mr Johnson?' Hammond asked.

The woman answered with a sharp nod. Her body language gave the impression that she was not interested in what Hammond had to tell, but her piercing gaze belied her desperation to know details.

'Mr Johnson has not been seen since last Wednesday, so we are just checking his home to establish his whereabouts.' Hammond wanted to appear open. Experience had taught him that the elder inquisitives were often a good source of information.

'I haven't seen him either,' the woman offered. 'But I've seen her.'

'Are you referring to Ms Taylor? Mr Johnson's partner?'

'I don't know her name, but she could be his partner. She never had the decency to introduce herself, but she certainly behaves as if she owns the place. She was here yesterday.'

'Yes, Ms Taylor is currently helping us with our enquiries. She's also looking after Mr Johnson's dog for the time being.'

The woman didn't answer, just nodded as her eyes scanned Hammond. Then she said, 'So, what do you think has happened to him? Has he done a runner?'

Hammond shook his head. 'I don't think so. What do you think? Is he a private kind of man?'

The neighbour was enjoying his attention, and she leant on the fence as she deliberated. 'Yes, but he is ok. Bit quiet but friendly. He would say hello, or help me cut my lawn sometimes. My husband didn't like him, but then my Eric wasn't very sociable anyway. I'm Ellie, Ellie Winters.'

Hammond offered his hand to shake, which she accepted and then retracted her hand back over the fence.

'My Eric doesn't live here now. He had a stroke last year, so he is in that nursing home up the hill.'

Hammond listened respectfully but was aware that Edwards was fidgeting. He bade the neighbour goodbye and thanked her for her patience.

'It may be necessary for us to pop back, but I will ask Mischa, Ms Taylor, to make herself known if you like, just so you are aware of any comings and goings.'

The neighbour called him back. 'Mischa, did you say? I know Mischa. She's the dark-haired woman.'

Hammond turned back. 'Yes, that's right.'

'But she's not the girlfriend. No, Mischa is the friend. I meant the other one. The short, skinny one. She was round there yesterday, tipped a bundle of paper in the recycling bin then left the lid to flap about. I had to go and squash it down to stop all the rubbish blowing all over the road.'

Hammond stopped. 'I'm sorry, the short lady?'

'Yes, the silver-haired one.'

CHAPTER SIX

Elijah had no idea how long they had been shuffling forwards. The other's man's body had been pressed closely against his back as they tentatively took a step forward blindly, but eventually he was told to stop. Elijah tried to listen. There was no sound other than their shallow breathing due to the poor air quality. The atmosphere was humid and dank.

The other man stopped and moved further away from Elijah. There was the sound of rustling before Elijah's eyes were blinded by an intense light. He yelped and covered his eyes whilst they adjusted to the sudden brightness.

The man adjusted his head torch and waited for Elijah to look towards him, then he spoke.

'It's not an easy walk, so stay close to me and follow my lead. I strongly suggest that you do not try to leave me. We are almost one hundred feet underground. If you leave me, it will be very easy to get lost, and chances are you will never find your way back. Do you understand?'

Elijah swallowed, tasting grit and mould. He regretted throwing his phone earlier; it would have given him enough light to fumble his way back if he was able to lose his companion. Instead, he was reliant on a stranger with likely hostile intentions towards him.

He nodded, signalling his compliance. His body felt weak and drained of energy, even though his mind was screaming at him to run or fight. But Elijah knew any attempt would be hopeless. He had no idea where he was, who this other person was, or why he had been brought to such a hellhole. He was frightened and his body was shaking despite the almost suffocating heat. The dark walls of earth seemed to be pressing against him and he felt he was slowly being crushed.

His companion squeezed past Elijah. He had removed his hood, and now Elijah got an idea of the other person. The light briefly beamed down on his face and affected an almost skeletal profile, before he moved in front and became just a dark form.

They continued forward, one step at a time, blindly following the path ahead, which was sometimes soft underfoot, at other times littered with what felt like stones or gravel. Above them, the ceiling became higher to accommodate a wide yellow tube that was strung up by red rubber cables. Chicken wire lined the ceiling and the upper sides of the walls.

Elijah recognised the system; there would be ventilation shafts somewhere. He paid attention to the flexible duct above them, looking for fans that he could possibly use to gauge where openings would be. It was impossible to know where they were, or how long they had been shuffling like this. Chances were, it would be dark above ground now, so he had no choice but to follow.

Elijah held up his hands to steady himself when the walls appeared to narrow towards him. He thought he felt brick or stone. At one point, sickness overwhelmed him, the air quality changed, and he stopped to vomit. The man in front waited, not speaking, then they continued forward.

'How far are we going?' Elijah needed to know what was happening. The panic was changing into a rage that made him confident.

The other man did not speak. Soon after, Elijah felt their pace increasing and the tunnel appeared to widen, the air changed. He tasted loam on his tongue. The feeling of damp air clung to his skin.

The man stopped. 'Stay here,' he directed. Then he advanced.

Elijah went to follow, panic rising suddenly as the darkness quickly descended around him again.

'STOP!' the man shouted. The bellow bounced off the walls and seemed to reverberate.

Elijah stopped. His heart was hammering in his chest and he became conscious that he was gasping. Time passed, and Elijah had no idea whether he had been alone minutes or hours. He had no concept of time; he might have blacked out leaning against the wall. He didn't know. His senses were completely overwhelmed.

Suddenly there was light all around him. It flickered several times then became steadier and stronger. Then he heard the padding of footsteps on soft ground, and his companion stood a few feet away.

'Follow me,' he was instructed.

The two men followed the tunnel that was now widening. A hatch door had been opened in front of them, and the man stooped as he entered a small chamber. Elijah followed and found himself in a small room that was lit by a naked bulb hanging down from the ceiling. Against a concrete wall was a small table and two chairs.

Elijah rushed towards the bottles of water that were on the table. He ripped the lid off one without asking and glugged the water in greedy gulps, almost snorting the liquid in his haste to rehydrate. The other man sat in a chair and watched with a strange smile.

'Now we talk,' he said.

CHAPTER SEVEN

Hammond did not like inconsistencies. In all the years he had spent policing, he still could not understand why people had to lie. Often, the motive was to gain in some way, but ultimately it was not to their advantage. Lies were almost always uncovered, along with the credibility of the people he was trying to help.

As they drove to Susan Maxwell's home, Hammond was speaking his thoughts aloud. Occasionally, he thumped the steering wheel, much to Edwards' perplexity.

'It doesn't mean she lied. The neighbour said she was there yesterday, so possibly your visit to her on Thursday prompted her to act,' he suggested.

Hammond nodded. 'Either way, the neighbour said that she is there often. Susan told me that she doesn't see Elijah that often, so the two accounts are not consistent. Why did Susan give the impression she and Elijah don't see each other often?'

Edwards shrugged. 'Maybe she has a jealous partner and wants to spare his insecurities.'

Hammond looked sideways at Edwards. 'No, I'm not convinced.' He sighed. 'Well, we'll give her the opportunity to explain.'

He paused whilst he stopped at a junction and noticed a burger van parked in a lay-by further down the road. The reminder that it was past lunchtime tempted him to stop, but he resisted the urge to rest until he was satisfied that they were making progress.

'It makes you wonder why we do this job,' he mused.

Edwards attempted to cheer him up. 'You only have a few weeks left of it. Just think, in a few weeks' time you can put your feet up and do what you like!'

Hammond's answer remained unspoken.

Susan Maxwell's attitude was less friendly than on Hammond's first visit, but she invited both men into the house and sat down, evidently willing to cooperate.

'I didn't mean to be dishonest,' she explained in response to Hammond's near accusation. 'Elijah and I have a complicated connection. We are close but we don't get involved in one another's lives.'

'Involved enough to go to his house and rummage through his private papers in his loft?' Hammond leaned forward, defying her to deny it.

Susan flushed. Instinctively, she rubbed her forearm where a deep scratch was evident.

'I'm not sure what you are implying...' she began then stopped as she read Hammond's expression of disbelief. 'Okay, yes, I did let myself in to Elijah's house, but I swear I have nothing to do with his disappearance. I genuinely have no idea where he is.'

Hammond leaned back in the chair but studied her as she spoke. He believed her. 'You need to explain to us what you took, and why you had the need to dispose of it.'

Susan looked offended by Hammond's patronising tone, but she resisted arguing. Instead, she focused more on Edwards.

'Elijah and I have an unspoken agreement. I help him out financially, but it is not something that we share with anyone, partly because it is no-one's business, but also because I like to think that, by being discreet, I am allowing Elijah to have some dignity.'

Hammond accepted this. 'Did you have an official agreement to support him financially as part of your divorce settlement?'

Susan shook her head. 'No, we parted amicably. There was no need for us to split assets or such like, because we agreed he took with him what he wanted or what he had bought himself. I took what was originally mine or what I had bought. There was no fuss or disagreement.'

'So, how is this relevant to your visit to Elijah's house on Sunday? What was it you took from the house?'

Susan shifted slightly. 'Payment receipts that I had helped him with.'

Edwards raised an eyebrow. 'I'm guessing large sums were involved?'

Susan hesitated. 'Not as such. I loaned him ten thousand towards the deposit for his bungalow, but it was a loan. If you check his bank statements, you will see that he repays me in monthly instalments.'

Hammond fidgeted in his chair. 'I'm confused. Whilst this is interesting, it doesn't really explain why you took receipts from Elijah's attic. Surely no-one would have been interested in checking this information if, like you say, the bank statements show he is repaying you. But even if he didn't, none of this explains where he is right now or why no-one can account for his disappearance.'

He changed his tone. 'There's is something you are not telling us, so I suggest you tell us everything you can to stop wasting our time. We have reason to believe that Elijah has been receiving threats. He could be in danger, so stop messing around!'

Susan flushed again. For several seconds she studied the room, but eventually she relented. 'Ok. Yes, I know that Elijah had been getting threatening messages. He told me about them. They were not so bad at first, just spiteful, angry accusations that he couldn't make sense of.'

'He showed them to you?'

Susan nodded.

'So, you advised him?'

'No. Not at first. I suggested Elijah should go to the Police, but he said that violence hadn't been specifically threatened so the Police wouldn't treat it seriously. Plus, he didn't know what he had done to provoke the messages. Perhaps stupidly, I suggested he reply, asking them to clarify and to apologise if he had caused offence.'

'Do you know how he replied?'

'By email. Eventually, he got a reply back. They told him that he had to pay for his crimes; those were the exact words.' Susan hesitated, then became more earnest in her justification. 'I'm a girl who has been brought up surrounded by wealth, so if someone tells me I have to pay, well, automatically, I think they mean money…' She opened her hands wide.

Edwards groaned, predicting her next words. 'So, you told Elijah to pay the sender of the threats money?'

Susan nodded.

'How much?'

'I told Elijah to offer them twenty thousand in cash.'

Hammond ignored Edwards' muttered blasphemous exclamation. 'And… they agreed?'

'Yes, they told Elijah to leave it by the adult gym equipment at Hythe green.'

Hammond was incredulous. 'I'm guessing they took the money and then the threats continued?'

Susan was silent. After a minute, she nodded, but looked down as she wrung her hands, as if finally realising the enormity of her stupidity. When she looked up, she had tears in her eyes.

'Ok, so the papers from the loft, these were connected somehow?' Edwards asked.

Susan nodded. 'Yes. Printouts of the emails, photographs of the money drop. We even waited for the bag to be collected and took photographs of everyone who came near, but whoever it was came through the trees from the canal path so we didn't see the bag being taken. Elijah wrote everything down. He wanted to find out who it was but, more importantly, what he had done wrong to cause such hatred towards him.'

Hammond frowned. 'Did you read all his notes?' Susan shook her head. 'So, you don't know if he was successful in identifying his accuser?'

Hammond's headache had crept down to his shoulders. He felt nauseous. The feeling of helplessness was beginning to overwhelm him.

Very quietly, he asked, 'These were the notes that you took from the attic and discarded?'

Susan nodded.

*

Edwards drove back to the station. The two men were hungry and tired, but the sense of urgency overrode their need to eat. Hammond was anxious to get as many resources allocated as possible.

'I need more manpower,' he explained to Morris. 'There's a credible threat here, and we have wasted too much time already.'

He was angry, but couldn't direct the blame at anyone but himself. Since Mischa's visit to the station on Thursday, he had not responded with urgency. Instead, he had treated Elijah's disappearance as a cause for concern. The first twenty-four hours had been crucial, but Hammond had lain in bed nursing a headache, having left the responsibility with the Missing Persons' team. He had let Elijah down.

Morris listened attentively to Hammond's update. 'The CCTV footage has come in, but from what I understand, you requested for footage from 6pm on Wednesday evening. When did the money drop-off happen?'

Hammond checked his notebook. 'Wednesday, March 20th. Four weeks ago.'

Morris sighed. 'Well, I guess we could see how the first lot of footage captures that area, but I agree it's unlikely so there may be no point in requesting for more footage from that date. The view from the council offices to the gym equipment is partially obscured and quite a distance away, so even if the camera did get an image, by the time it's been zoomed in, the image will be too pixelated for clarity to identify the person moving the bag. And then, of course, who is to tell that it is not some opportunistic thief?'

Morris considered quietly. 'Susan Maxell hasn't helped us, but at least now we know a bit more background. I agree we need to act with some urgency. I can give you two more detectives as extra manpower for the remainder of the week. DS Williams is pursuing the request for the library's computer history to be accessed, and I've pre-warned the tech team that there's material to be treated as priority for them to check. But you're working blind.'

Hammond agreed. He ran his hand through his hair, realising how thin it felt. Morris studied him as if reading his mind.

'You're not looking well,' he said. 'I think your imminent retirement is something of a blessing for you.' He paused. 'If you want to stop a little early, I am willing to put in a request for health reasons.'

Hammond stood up straighter. 'No, thank you. I'd like to see this one through.'

Morris accepted this with a slight smile. 'Ok. I do understand the need to resolve this, but before you start blaming yourself for failing to act quickly enough, bear in mind there is nothing to indicate that Elijah Johnson is a vulnerable person or the victim of a crime. I agree that the suggested threat is enough to treat this as a potential abduction, but there is still a possibility that Elijah has simply gone off somewhere without telling anyone.'

Morris paused, noting Hammond's dubious expression. 'Well, let's aim to have this wrapped up quickly. Hopefully, the appeals via the media will bear fruit.'

*

The afternoon of Monday, 15th April, was chaotic. The activity had increased significantly, and it was a challenge to think straight. Hammond was running on adrenaline. He couldn't eat and would forget to drink even if a cup was placed before him. Interviews with members of the Squash Club Elijah frequented had provided no new information, and reports of possible sightings of Elijah had to be responded to and processed, even though the majority of witness accounts proved unreliable. CCTV footage had been limited, although it had shown Elijah's route to the bus stop. The Stagecoach bus company's provision of surveillance on the bus, however, was a little more helpful.

'There are five closed circuit television cameras on the outside of the bus and two inside.' DS Williams addressed Hammond and Edwards. 'There is clear footage of Elijah boarding the bus at 18.25. He walks towards the back here. Several seconds later, he is seen talking to someone whose back is to the camera. They're wearing a hood, so their features are obscured and it's impossible to tell what gender they are, but we see them sit next to Elijah. There seems to be some interaction, although the other person doesn't appear to be talking at any time. But they are sitting very close to Elijah on the seat, unnecessarily so, unless they know each other. Elijah is fidgeting, though, and tapping the handrail as if he is agitated. Then they are seen disembarking together. Elijah stops to talk to the driver before they get off – only three minutes later, two stops from when he boarded.'

All three men stared at the large television screen in the briefing room.

'You can see the footage taken from the cameras on the outside of the bus which shows Elijah and his mystery companion get off. Behind them, you can see the cafe where there are several people seated near the window. They could be potential witnesses.' Williams spoke with a tone of optimism.

'They're standing still whilst the bus moves off,' Edwards spoke up. 'Where do they go from there? There's no way of knowing.'

Hammond leaned closer towards the screen. The headache was compromising his vision. 'But why are they standing still? Think about it. You get off a bus; if you are going somewhere specific, you are more likely to keep walking, unless you intend to cross the road to directly opposite where the bus stopped, to go to a place very close to that particular stop or, perhaps more likely, wait for another bus.'

He turned around and faced Williams. 'What is the next bus that stops there after the 102 leaves?'

CHAPTER EIGHT

Respite for Hammond came at 5.30pm when Lois Dunn phoned. It was a pleasant surprise to hear from his ex-colleague and he told her so.

'I saw the appeal for the missing man. How are you getting on?'

'Slowly.' Hammond's brief answer made it obvious he had little confidence in a positive outcome.

'What have you got so far?' she asked.

Hammond briefed her, surprised that she was taking a personal interest in their investigations despite the fact that she was 70 miles away. *She misses us,* he thought.

'What about the girlfriend? What's her background?'

Hammond mused for a few minutes. 'Well, she has been his partner for just over eighteen months. She works in estate management'

'Estate management? So, she would have access to lots of buildings then?'

Hammond laughed. 'Good thinking, but I don't suspect her of abducting her boyfriend. There's nothing for her to gain by attracting our attention.' He changed the subject. 'How are you doing there?'

There was a long sigh. 'We are snowed under. I expect you are aware of the number of random stabbings in London. It's crazy. I haven't gone home much in the last month.'

Hammond sympathised. The number of killings in London in 2018 had risen to its highest level for a decade, and appeared to be on an upward trend.

Dunn changed the subject. 'Only three weeks to go! Are you excited?'

Hammond's retirement appeared to be a cause for celebration to everyone but himself. 'Not really,' he admitted. 'To be honest, I have no idea what I'll do with myself. However, at least I'll get the chance to see you at the party. You're still coming?'

'I wouldn't miss it for the world.' Dunn's tone relaxed as she conveyed her sincerity. Their respect for one another was mutual. They'd had many disagreements over the years, but with Hammond's stubbornness and Dunn's tenacity, they had concluded many cases successfully. The call ended and Hammond returned to the meeting. Edwards looked up and studied him as he entered the room. He frowned as Hammond misjudged the distance between the chair and the table, bashing his hip.

'Go home,' he said. 'I'll update you if there is any significant progress.'

Reluctantly, Hammond obliged. For some inexplicable reason, he considered that if he were a wild animal, all he would do right now would be to curl into a ball in a corner and allow himself to drift off into a never-ending sleep.

*

Paul was not in when Hammond arrived home, but surprisingly he had left him a plate of cooked food on the table, wrapped in tinfoil. It was a thoughtful gesture.

He looked for a note wondering whether Paul had returned home to his wife but, not finding any, ate the mashed potatoes and beef mince with relish.

Paul returned to the flat before 9pm, but by that time Hammond had already gone to bed.

*

Detective Sergeants Edwards and Williams shared their progress with Hammond as he entered the office just before 8am on Tuesday morning.

'Elijah had left his bag of groceries on the bus, and luckily the driver had retained it as lost property.'

'It's definitely Elijah's?' Hammond asked.

'Yes, another passenger saw him leave the shopping as he got up from his seat. He ignored her when she called him, so she presumed he hadn't heard her, but the driver was told when she saw that keys had been left attached to the shopping bag handle.'

Hammond's head tilted to one side in a typical evaluation pose. 'Odd. Where is the shopping now?'

'It's being collected now whilst the driver is being interviewed. I asked the station manager to email pictures. The plastic handle of the bag had been slotted into the key ring quite deliberately.'

Hammond frowned. 'Why would he do that?' He peered closer at the picture. 'They look like door keys. And that is a Dacia remote key, which will likely fit the car I saw in Elijah's garage.' He paused. 'Elijah was wearing a jacket. Why didn't he put his keys in his pocket?' He looked up at Edwards. 'Do you think he was trying to communicate something?'

Edwards offered a smile. 'Please take my shopping home for me?'

Hammond ignored the sarcasm and continued to study the image before him. 'What about the key fob?'

Edwards shrugged. 'Just those mini plastic key fobs. There's his Tesco Clubcard fob, the library fob, and another marketing type for something called *Cambridge Virtuosos*.'

Their attention was diverted by a call from the tech team. Edwards listened to the caller, jotting down notes and nodding occasionally. He ended the call and offered an apologetic smile.

'The hostile messages sent to Elijah were sent using a burner Gmail account, so there is no identifying information on the user. The tech team couldn't locate the original IP address, so they suspect an email client had been installed on the sender's system to connect to a virtual private network. But on the plus side, there was no malware attached to the email which, from our point of view, suggests that the sender was someone with a genuine grievance rather than a crime organisation sending random messages as a scam.'

'In other words, the sender is genuinely hostile but can't be traced?' Hammond sighed.

'Not quickly or easily, no.'

'But they can tell us if more stealth emails are being sent to Elijah's account?' Hammond paused whilst he sorted out his thoughts. 'We don't know for sure that the sender is involved in Elijah's disappearance. Have there been any more messages received?'

'There haven't been any received since 25th March.'

Hammond nodded. 'It could suggest that they know Elijah is not receiving messages hence they are not writing to him. Or they are satisfied with the money he paid them on the 20th and don't intend to pursue their campaign.'

'But they did write once after the 20th.'

Hammond stroked his chin as he considered the possibilities. 'Maybe they were just trying their luck. Elijah didn't reply after the 10th April, so perhaps they gave up.'

Frustrated, he slapped his hands on the table. 'It's all maybes and possibilities! When are we going to make any bloody progress?' Hammond forced himself to calm. 'Ok, what if we send an email back to them?'

Edwards responded hesitantly, 'We could... but saying what?'

Hammond was at impasse. If he contacted the hostile email messenger offering more money, it would possibly tempt them out of hiding, but there was no guarantee they were responsible for Elijah's absence. If they were, then sending a message pretending to be from Elijah could endanger him further if they suspected they were being played.

Hammond shook his head. 'I don't know what to do,' he admitted. Suddenly Hammond felt old. He was an old dog who couldn't chase his own tail.

'Understandably, the AKAE unit cannot act until we are sure that we are dealing with a kidnap,' DS Williams updated them as he read replies from the Anti-Kidnap and Extortion Team.

Hammond nodded. 'Well, we will keep them updated and follow their advice. In the meantime, how do they suggest we proceed?'

'To continue as we are, cautiously.'

Hammond was not sure such advice was helpful at this stage. He needed direction, and in that moment he knew that he was not functioning as an effective police officer. Once, he would have known exactly what to do in a situation like this, but now he couldn't think straight. He sat thoughtfully for several minutes, then he looked up decisively.

'Ok. This is what we'll do. We will not write to the sender of the stealth e-mails. Let's concentrate on what we do know and continue to gather as much intelligence as we can. Employ foot soldiers on the streets to circulate Elijah's description, gather any intelligence from potential witnesses and chase up any leads, no matter how implausible they may seem. We need to be thorough and transparent in all our dealings. Have we got any confirmation that Elijah boarded any bus from the stop where he had disembarked the first bus? Chase that up as a priority, and we will follow where that trail leads. We just have to accept that there is no shortcut to this; it has to take as long as it takes, but we must use every available second to our advantage.'

'What about the background checks?' Williams spoke up.

Hammond surveyed the Detective Sergeant. Tall, slim, with a calm and gentle manner, he was the youngest amongst them, possibly in his early thirties. He was enthusiastic and methodical. Hammond did not know the man well, but already he felt reassured that this younger detective was a good asset to the team.

'Yes, continue them, please. Even if they are just basic checks of anyone whom we know to have come into contact with Elijah. If there is a person out for revenge, there may be link that can be traced.' Hammond looked apologetically at his colleague. 'It could be a waste of time but I'm grasping at straws right now.'

Williams nodded and concentrated his attention on the computer in front of him.

When Elijah's groceries were brought to the office, Hammond and Edwards concentrated on the contents: a stale brown baguette, pate, porridge oats, and a bottle of beer. The shopping bag was a new plastic one. They then examined the keys, taking each one off the ring and positioning them side by side on the table. The plastic key cards were also examined – Elijah's faded Tesco Clubcard barcode; his library account card; and a marketing mini plastic fob.

It wouldn't be difficult to check the keys connected to Elijah's house locks. 'Why would he abandon them so obviously?' Hammond questioned aloud. Then he saw it. He saw why.

Picking up the last plastic card key fob, he ran his finger over the indent where the card had been bent towards one end. *Cambridge Virtuo*. He turned the card and read the letters separated by the crease.

'This is why,' Hammond said. 'He was sending out an SOS'.

CHAPTER NINE

'I'm now convinced we are looking at abduction,' Hammond updated Superintendent Morris.

Their investigation was not picking up pace. Despite the team effort appealing for potential witnesses, completing background checks, and interviewing the driver of the 102 bus, Elijah's journey appeared to have come to a standstill half a mile from where he had last been seen.

'The perpetrator is likely to be this unidentified figure in the hooded jumper. We've studied the bus surveillance footage more closely and now believe that all this time Elijah has been attempting to communicate. First, there was the SOS message using the key fob. The surveillance on the bus is very sketchy, but I've played it back several times and Edwards agrees that it looks as if Elijah is tapping quickly three times on the handrail in front of him, then pausing, then swiping three times. It's not exactly Morse code, but it could be interpreted as an attempt to replicate the SOS code.

'That isn't conclusive, of course, but the driver remembers Elijah, which we believe was a deliberate attempt on Elijah's part to communicate,' Hammond went on. 'Before he got off the bus, he spoke to the driver as if he knew him, saying, "Thank you, Kartee!", even though the driver didn't recognise him. Then, as he stepped off the bus, Elijah called over his shoulder, "Hope all goes well for Persephone".'

'That doesn't sound like the behaviour of a man in trouble.' Superintendent Morris looked dubious. But, after a few seconds of thought, he nodded. 'Yes, I can see where you are heading. Hecates rescued Persephone when she was abducted by Hades.'

'Exactly,' Hammond agreed. 'Bearing in mind he writes trivia quiz questions, it fits. It's quite a basic clue, but if it hadn't been, we wouldn't have understood his attempt!'

Morris smiled at the veiled insult. 'It's progress,' he confirmed. 'Are there any leads on where they went next?'

Hammond flattened out a map on Morris desk. 'Unless they were collected by a vehicle waiting at the car park of the miniature railway, there are several possibilities. They could have used any of the footpaths alongside the canal. But there have been no reported sightings of Elijah after he got off the bus.'

He pointed to an area of woodland further west along the canal path. 'To avoid too many witnesses, they may have avoided the major paths and followed the route heading uphill onto the escarpment of the North Downs – labelled here as The Roughs. But, logically thinking, this is not where you would take someone if they were unwilling, as there are too many opportunities to run off. The same goes if they were heading to the housing developments nearby. So, I'm thinking it's more likely that they were collected at the cafe car park and driven elsewhere.'

Hammond straightened up and looked at Morris. 'It's all ifs, buts, and maybes, but it's a start. All the vehicles that were parked at the cafe and the miniature railway are being identified, and their routes from the cafe traced. There weren't many at that time in the evening. Other than the staff's vehicles, there are only five that need tracing. We have a team of Special Constables doing door-to-door enquiries in surrounding areas to find potential witnesses. It's a neighbourhood watch area, which may be to our advantage. If there were any unfamiliar cars parked outside the houses, they would be noted.'

Superintendent Morris listened and studied the map before him. 'What about the areas you have not marked?'

Hammond circled a section with his finger. 'This is an industrial development with eleven businesses renting units there. We are sending officers to check any empty storage units, but it's a long shot. The walk from the cafe to the development is too conspicuous along the main road, unless they drove there. But, again...' Hammond shook his head as he considered the absence of logic in such a move. 'If you are going to take someone against their will on a public bus, then drive a short distance from the bus stop, why not abduct them using a car in the first place?'

'Crazy people do crazy things,' Morris muttered unhelpfully.

'It begs the question whether Elijah has not been abducted and is deliberately creating a diversion,' Hammond wondered.

'But from what? I agree the whole idea is ludicrous so far, but he has communicated a plea for help so we must at least try to make sense of what we do have. This area here – The Roughs and surrounding MOD land – from what I remember, there are numerous old bunkers and tunnels in this area. I suggest you get search teams deployed to check around there. The fact that Elijah has been so compliant suggests coercion. If he believes he is protecting his ex-wife or girlfriend, that would explain why he is allowing himself to be shepherded.'

Morris sighed heavily and gazed out the window. 'Of course, the question remains as to why Elijah is being targeted. Has there been any progress with researching his background?'

Hammond hesitated before answering, but eventually his frustration got the better of him and he spoke more openly than his better sense directed.

'We are a small team, working flat out to locate Elijah, therefore our focus has been concentrated on recovering rather than researching. If we had more resources, then it would be a different story.'

Morris turned and raised an eyebrow. 'I am limited on what I can offer; you're the senior investigator on this one. You have your priorities as I have mine. My priority is to oversee several serious cases that are happening at the same time. In the last three days we have had an attempted murder, a violent rape by an unknown assailant, and the aggravated burglary that happened in the home of an elderly victim. Every DCI is working flat out on other cases. You should know, Wallace, that no investigation is less worthy of resolution than another. Every case has a victim that needs closure. '

Hammond nodded. The despair was mutual. 'You're right, of course. I'll deploy search teams and keep you updated on any progress.'

As Hammond left the office of his senior officer, he had the ridiculous urge to cry.

*

Priorities. What takes priority right now? thought Hammond. *In three weeks, Paul and a new start in life will become my focus, but right now, what should take precedence?*

He looked across at Edwards, again absorbed in tapping and swiping the screen on his phone. The man was at work, yet evidently the harmony of his personal life was compromised by being there. Did that mean that the preservation of others' lives should be at the cost of their own loved ones' happiness?

Hammond chose to ignore Edwards' distraction. It was going to be a long day, so there might be few opportunities to sort his personal life out. For the next few minutes, Hammond reckoned, the man should be allowed to put his family first.

The background checks on Mischa and Susan proved to be un-illuminating. Their employment history, marital status, and financial standing had been verified, and neither had any criminal history, but this was not unexpected considering that the checks had simply been precautionary. The search teams had been deployed to search The Roughs, but Hammond suspected it would be a painstaking operation. With such a vast area, it would take several days.

He had briefly researched the area, which was rich in history, and it would have been interesting to learn more in other circumstances. He looked at the map and tried to ignore the feeling of helplessness overwhelm him. If Elijah was there, Hammond still had no idea why. And, worse, he didn't know whether the destination was simply a potential prison or not. It was now five days since Elijah had been seen, so there was a chance that the man had simply walked to his own grave.

*

It was past half ten that evening when Hammond finally stepped through the doorway of his apartment. He was disheartened, having had no progress to report for the day. As he had driven home, he had tried to imagine what his father would had said if he were alive. It was no secret that Hammond had become a police officer to gain the approval of Hammond Senior, who had been an avid fan of a British police procedural television series from the 1950s, based on the real-life memoirs of Scotland *Yard* detective Robert *Fabian*. Many evenings in Hammond's childhood had been spent listening to his father recount with rapture how cases were solved using the combined intelligence of forensic psychiatry, graphology, or pathology.

There had been no opportunity for Hammond to share his own investigations, unfortunately, as his father had died before he had graduated from Police College in 1977. But he liked to think that his father was somehow aware of his career.

Patience. That was the only answer his father could have given him. Be patient. During the forty years of his career, Hammond had encountered many days when it seemed as if no progress had been made, when an investigation had too many leads all pointing to various directions. It was too easy to try to follow every lead, instead of waiting to see which route was the most viable. Being patient and accepting that some days would be better spent waiting for the truth to reveal itself, was the only way to get through the frustration of what appeared to be a lack of progress.

As he shut the door, Hammond became aware that Paul had been waiting for him. The look of relief on his son's face was too apparent as he ventured further into the apartment.

'I need your opinion.' Paul smiled meekly, reminiscent of the days when he had asked for help with his homework.

Hammond sat down, relieved that at last his son wanted to share his woes, but aware he felt rather nervous as to what was about to be confided.

Ten minutes after his son had started speaking, Hammond felt a mixture of excitement and confusion.

'Jenny has asked me to be the father of her biological baby.'

'Jenny?' Hammond queried. 'But she's gay! Isn't she? Are you telling me that after all these years you are going to be a couple?'

Hammond spoke with utter disbelief. Jenny had been a close friend to Paul for fifteen years; so close that Hammond had considered Jenny as a daughter. Their affection was mutual but the relationship was complex, because Jenny was complex. She was the most elusive and mysterious character Hammond had ever known.

He had no idea where she had come from or who her family was. One day she had appeared in their lives, and had shown no sign of exiting. She would pop up out of the blue for a quick conversation and then disappear for months, sometimes years without a word, before appearing again as if they had seen each other only hours before. The only certainty Hammond had about Jenny was that she was a lesbian, and had been ever since he had known her. He had counselled her many times following break-ups, but she had always coped as a free spirit and was not someone that would settle in one place.

Paul reacted as if his father had suggested he had committed an act of incest.

'Of course not! Jenny wants a baby, but she doesn't want to have just anyone's sperm, she asked me if I would...' Paul blushed and coughed, as if the words had got stuck in his throat.

'Donate?' Hammond offered.

'Yes, exactly.'

Hammond smiled, realising the thought of becoming a grandfather was appealing. 'It's quite an honour to be asked. But what do you think about it?'

Paul shuffled his body round on the sofa so that he was looking forward rather than facing his father directly. He was embarrassed, his face was flushed, his eyes fixed on his hands that were clasped in his lap.

'I want to be a father, that's no secret,' he said eventually, 'but I'd hoped that Bettina would be open to the idea of us having our own one day. Instead, when I told her of Jenny's proposition, she encouraged me to go ahead, saying she admired Jenny's feminist ideals by deliberately omitting a man in her plans. I had the whole lecture: how modern women do not need men in their lives; how children do not need to identify gender relations... well, you know how she goes on...' Paul smiled at Hammond's short laugh.

'Well, anyway, I said I would prefer us to have a child together. I think I used the term "like normal parents", to which she raged that I was prehistoric in my nuclear family ideals. Then she stated that she never wants to be a mother.' He paused before continuing, 'I don't know what's worse: knowing that my wife doesn't want to have a child with me, or having her encourage me into having a child with another woman as if I was no more than a sperm donor that can be passed around.'

'I don't think that is why Jenny asked you, Paul,' Hammond told him. 'I know how much she loves and respects you. It's likely that she asked you because she wants to share the ultimate connection with you.'

Paul looked at his father with such an expression of hurt that Hammond automatically circled his arm around his son and embraced him. It did not matter to him that Paul was a grown man of thirty-three years; he was his child that needed comforting.

They stayed like that for several minutes, until Paul moved away, patting his father's hands awkwardly.

'I don't know how to advise you.' Hammond spoke first. 'I think you would make a wonderful father, and all that really matters is that your child is loved and well cared for. I have the same faith in Jenny, but I have to admit, I cannot see Bettina as the maternal type. I guess you need to decide whether you love Bettina enough to sacrifice your dreams of being a father, or decide that you can be happy elsewhere, having a family with some-one else.'

Paul nodded and sighed. 'I think I've always known that Bettina has never been as committed to me as I have been to her. For a while, it was enough, but now… now I realise that I want to have children and I am not willing to give that dream up – at least, not for someone who doesn't respect me in the same way.'

Hammond patted his son on his knee as he stood up. 'Then you've answered your own question,' he said.

Chapter Ten

When Lieutenant-Colonel John Brown of the Royal
Staff Corps of Field Engineers devised a strategy for the
defence of the south coast against Napoleonic invasion
in 1804, he was convinced that the Romney Marshlands
was an area that would be inundated by enemy infiltra-
tion. Hence, he devised the Royal Military Canal – a
twenty-eight mile staggered stretch of water, with artil-
lery batteries placed every 500 yards, and additional
towers built to protect the sluices. Lieutenant-Colonel
Brown's idea was effective, even though it proved to be
unnecessary; the canal did not see any military action.

Instead, it was used to control the smuggling of wool
and contraband from Romney Marsh, further aided by
the Guardhouses which were constructed at each bridge.
Further reinforcements were added over a century later,
with concrete pillboxes and underground bunkers built
as preparation for threatened German invasion during
the Second World War.

With an area so rich in military history, there were
the inevitable reminders set in the local environment.
Hammond knew there were several disused bunkers,
but he had not accounted for the fact that many of the
old constructions still existed. When the confirmed
report came in on Tuesday morning that Elijah's mobile
phone had been found at the entrance of an old

munitions underground storage hidden on the canal bank, his short-lived sense of relief quickly became hopelessness when it became apparent that the storage facility had not been blocked off as originally believed.

'Search teams checked the waters, but there was no sign of anyone having fallen into the water. There are members checking the banks, but we are not likely to need specialist underwater teams,' Edwards informed him. 'Elijah's phone was found actually inside the entrance structure. There is the usual graffiti and accumulation of rubbish, and despite being hidden by shrubbery, the munitions storage entrance is easily accessible. At first glance it looks like a small shelter, but when the dogs alerted a find, on closer examination it was apparent that the wall at the back of the old munitions storage had collapsed, exposing a small area that looks as if it progresses into a tunnel. It was deemed too unsafe to go any further.'

Hammond sighed. 'How sure are they that there is a tunnel behind the old wall?'

Edwards hesitated, unsure how to respond, and both men were silent for a while whilst they digested the possibility.

After a few minutes Edwards offered his considerations. 'If the wall had been built to block the tunnel before the area was used for storage, it's likely to have been there over two centuries ago, during which time the geography has changed. The land has shifted too much, and with the recent rainfall, it is not safe to enter any further, especially since we cannot know for sure that Elijah was taken into that area.'

Hammond looked at the photographs. 'The tunnel is still partially hidden, though. Can they tell whether the bricks were removed deliberately, or has it simply deteriorated and been open for a while?'

Edwards consulted his notes. 'There were some old wrappers just inside the entrance – crisp packets with a best before date of 2011. However, it doesn't look as if anyone has gone very far into it.'

Hammond sighed. 'But we have had rainfall since Wednesday. If the water levels have risen and damp has got in, then we wouldn't find any signs anyway. So, I assume search tactics are being reviewed as we speak?' He paused whilst he waited for confirmation. 'Ok, well we have Elijah's phone, which is a step forward. I agree that it may have been thrown back by Elijah deliberately as he was coerced into the tunnel. Since he has attempted to communicate up till now, it is plausible. It also explains why we didn't get a signal, I suppose.'

Hammond was thinking aloud, but then he turned back to Edwards. 'How quickly until we can get access to all the phone data?'

Williams called over, his head bent over the computer. 'It's being treated as priority. Hopefully, we will have something in a few hours.'

Hammond offered an unconvincing thumbs-up gesture as he walked to Superintendent Morris's office.

*

The Superintendent was not pleased. 'If we are to have specialist teams deployed, that is a huge expense that I may not be able to justify,' he said.

'We're having trouble locating any historical information of any tunnels in the area,' Hammond explained. 'It's going to take up many hours and manpower just to research it thoroughly, and I cannot guarantee it is necessary. However,' he leant forward on Morris's desk, 'if Elijah is in there, he could be in serious danger, and I can't sit back and let him rot when we could be strategising a rescue operation.'

Morris was quiet for a while. 'I need to make a phone call,' he said. 'In the meantime, research as best you can whilst you're waiting for the mobile phone to be examined. The local library has a museum, doesn't it? There may be some information on any underground defence networks in the area. I'd rather we look at the possibilities before we call in too many specialists. Have you checked with the girlfriend or the ex-wife to see if Elijah has contacted them?'

Hammond nodded. 'Elijah's mother has also been interviewed, but she has no information to offer either.'

Morris picked up the phone and waved Hammond out of the office. 'I'll speak with you in an hour.'

*

'Surely the Ministry of Defence would know more?' Alice's eyes widened in disbelief as Hammond explained the reason for his visit. But she was eager to be of assistance, and took him to the local history section where she selected several maps of Hythe from the 1800s.

'There was the school of Musketry sited here.' She tapped her finger on a small map dated 1854. 'It's probable that they used the site you described as a storage area, but there is a tunnel further up the hill that was used by the Mackeson's brewery, and later as an air raid shelter. It goes along this road here. If there is a network of tunnels like you suggest, this could be another entrance.' She indicated a road north of the canal, then noticed Hammond was looking at an old railway map.

She shook her head slightly, causing her hair bun to wobble slightly. 'Those are old tunnels from the old railway, but they are not likely to connect to these older tunnels we see in this map. They go into Saltwood and Sandling, but they are quite well known and heavily frequented. I also think they are blocked. I cannot see that they would connect to the canal.'

Hammond nodded; it made sense. He studied the old maps and drew rough copies in his notebook. Alice studied him.

'Is there really a chance that Mr Johnson was abducted?' she asked. 'It really doesn't seem possible. He is such a quiet, calm, normal person. I can't understand why anyone would want to kidnap him.' She flushed as Hammond turned his attention to her. 'It just seems so surreal, kidnapping him off a bus and taking him to a disused tunnel.'

Alice shook her head as if settling her imagination and trying to make sense of what Hammond had confided in her. 'It's just a bit theatrical.' She blushed again and fussed over the maps as she rearranged them in order and returned them to their files.

'Are there any old military documents that you don't have available in the library?' Hammond asked.

'I'm guessing the National Archives in Kew will offer most of what you need, but if you are limited on research time or manpower, Folkestone Library will have a greater selection in their archives. Otherwise, you can access the archive catalogue at Maidstone. But here the only other information is in the museum,' Alice answered. 'There is some archaeological material, a few bits relating to the Small Arms School, old military paraphernalia, like uniforms or weapons, but nothing that I know would help you.'

Hammond turned and perched on the edge of the table watching her. He noted she was not wearing a ring on her left hand. He was enjoying her company. He had only been in the library thirty minutes but was tempted to stay longer so he could continue talking to Alice. She had a calming effect on him.

Since he had been in her company, the sense of urgency within him had dwindled from panic to a more focused energy. He hesitated, wanting to invite her to lunch, but then reconsidered, noting that time couldn't be wasted however much he would have liked the opportunity to get to know her better. She turned and smiled at him shyly before enquiring if she was needed for anything else. He hesitated, the words forming on his tongue before he swallowed his proposed invitation and brought his attention back to work.

'Do you know of any military historians around here?' he said.

Alice cocked her head to one side and thought carefully, then she offered a rueful smile. 'I probably would have referred you to Mr Johnson,' she said with irony. 'He is quite knowledgeable.' Then she paused. 'Otherwise, there is Dominic. He is another of our regulars, and is quite friendly with Mr Johnson. He normally comes here on Tuesday afternoons, so you could speak to him today.'

She paused and hesitated before continuing, choosing her words carefully. 'Dominic is a lovely man, but you need to be careful how you approach him. He doesn't enjoy being looked at when he is being spoken to, so he will avoid eye contact with you, but it is not meant in an offensive way. He is extremely intelligent, absorbs knowledge like a sponge, and doesn't forget anything.'

Hammond nodded. 'It's ok,' he reassured her. 'I will be sensitive.'

She smiled broadly, her face reflecting the hue of pink from her fuchsia cardigan. 'Ok, I will point him out when he arrives, if you wish,' she offered.

He smiled back at her and accepted her offer, daring to prolong eye contact a moment longer than he needed to. *I'm an old man,* he thought to himself. *She's twenty years my junior; I have no chance.*

He excused himself and went outside to update Morris.

※

There was a spring in Hammond's step as he ventured back into the library. Morris had initiated specialist search teams to investigate the tunnel entrance, and the phone data from Elijah's mobile had been examined and was ready for review. The team was scheduled for a meeting within the hour.

There was a chance the investigation was making progress. Elijah's movements could possibly be tracked to God-knew-where, but Hammond hoped it was a step forward.

Alice caught his eye as he approached the reception area and glanced to her left quickly, indicating a very tall, dark-haired man in his early twenties. He was standing as if fixed to the carpet, his head bowed down, his arms rigid at his sides.

Hammond spoke to the bowed head, introduced himself, and explained his interest.

'I hope you can help me,' he said sincerely to Dominic.

'Over 80 thousand people go missing every year. One in 500 adults goes missing every 90 seconds,' Dominic told him. 'To be categorised as missing means that the person's whereabouts cannot be established and their disappearance is out of character.'

'That's correct,' Hammond acknowledged. 'Your friend Elijah is missing because we do not know where he is, and his friends and family are very worried about him.'

'Elijah may be the subject of a crime, or at risk of harm.'

'Yes, Dominic. That is why my colleagues and I are working hard to find him. I am hoping you can help me by telling me anything that Elijah may have shared with you, like his friends' names or where he liked to go.'

Dominic was rocking on his heels. Hammond looked for Alice, wondering whether she would count as an appropriate supervisor just in case his questions were later deemed to be inappropriate. He had no wish to interrogate the man and hesitated, wondering if he should proceed any further.

'Elijah is a nice man,' Dominic offered. 'I am his friend.'

'That's reassuring. What did you and Elijah like to talk about?'

Dominic had stopped rocking. His manner was calm, but his head remained bowed. 'Elijah doesn't always remember facts correctly, so I help him. He said that the Earth orbits around the sun, but actually the Earth orbits around the centre of the solar system mass, which is not at the sun's centre.'

'I see.' Hammond feigned understanding, then asked, 'Did Elijah share with you what he likes to look at when he is on the computer at the library?'

'He likes the online comprehensive encyclopaedias, almanacs, atlases, and dictionaries.'

'Does Elijah look at local history sites on the computer, or history books?'

Dominic stayed quiet.

Hammond paused, trying to gauge the young man's body language, then decided Dominic seemed calm enough to continue the conversation.

'We found Elijah's phone by a tunnel near the canal,' he explained. 'Did Elijah like looking at the old tunnels by the canal?'

'On 25th March, 1941, anti-aircraft batteries near RAF Lympne Airfield were looking out for a Focke-Wulf Condor aircraft,' Dominic replied. 'That is a German plane, but they were not allowed to shoot.'

Hammond frowned, unsure what the relevance was. He did not know how to proceed so he waited patiently, hoping for clarification. Having none, he moved slightly closer to Dominic and instantly became aware he had made a mistake. Dominic had begun rocking on his heels again, so Hammond stepped back and waited.

'Is that what Elijah was reading last Wednesday?' he asked.

'No. Last Wednesday Elijah was reading about a hotel.'

Hammond caught his breath. 'He was booking a hotel?'

Dominic shook his head. 'No, he was writing an email to the hotel.'

'Do you know what hotel?' Hammond's voice was light; he was trying to veil the extent of his interest. He could sense that Dominic's attention was waning.

'The tallest hotel in Zagreb, Croatia, is The Panorama Hotel.'

CHAPTER ELEVEN

'I wouldn't drink too much too quickly. It could make you sick, and I don't fancy you'll want to live amongst the stench of your own vomit. The shit will be bad enough.' The man leaned back in his chair nonchalantly.

Elijah looked at him. 'What do you mean live?'

The other man smirked but didn't reply.

The lack of response infuriated Elijah. This situation was incredible. He moved towards the other man with the intention of knocking him back in his chair. Elijah's bulk exceeded the other man's, but he was weak, ill prepared, and not as fit as his opponent, who reacted swiftly by sliding his foot under Elijah's advancing leg.

The action caused Elijah to fall head first, bashing his chin on the concrete floor. The man had risen from his chair and straddled Elijah, twisting his arm up his back. With his other hand, the man cupped Elijah's chin, forcing his head back, twisting his neck.

The pain in Elijah's shoulders was agonising. He attempted to call out but the words stuck in his throat as short gasps. He squeezed his eyes, sweat dripping down from his forehead. His chest was now being forced upwards from the floor as his attacker gripped his arm further back and up towards his shoulder blades. The pain increased and then he was released, gasping and rolled on his side in a foetal position. His arms clasped themselves against his chest to relieve the searing pain of torn ligaments under his arms.

The other man quietly returned to his chair and talked down at his victim.

'I get it, you're pissed off. There you were, heading home and then I popped up and spoilt your plans, but that's the way life is sometimes. Unexpected surprises can happen.'

Elijah swore and he heard laughter as a response. The man got up from the chair and stood for a minute, swinging his arms. 'I'll put the kettle on,' he said, as if the two of them were old friends.

'There's no milk, and no need to bother with sugar, so we'll have to have it black, but it's better than nothing.' The man started whistling whilst he arranged two tin cups and waited for the kettle to boil.

He caught Elijah looking at the kettle and he chuckled. 'Don't get any ideas about trying to scald me,' he said. 'You and I need to get along. Without me, you have no chance of getting out of here.' He paused. 'Alive anyway.'

He strained the tea bags and left them on a saucer by the kettle, then he walked back to the table and moved a chair, indicating Elijah seat himself.

Elijah did as expected, surprising himself by enjoying the tea. His stomach rumbled. His socks were damp, his trousers dusty, his hair damp with a mixture of sweat and moisture from the tunnel. He knew he looked frightened because he was, but inside there was a stirring of anger that was driving him on. He was going to get through this situation; he just didn't understand why he was in it.

'If you're lucky, I may even offer you dinner. But let's talk shop first, shall we?' The other man leaned forward, his legs spread apart. His forearms rested on his thighs.

'I've been asked to deliver you to my employer, but first we wait until he is ready. You're going to stay here for a bit until he gets here. Any attempts to fight me or cause trouble, will create far more problems for you than it will for me. You get it?'

Elijah stared at him furiously. 'What do you get for it?'

'Money. Lots of it, and I may even get a bit more if I can keep you alive until he gets here.'

'Who is your employer? And why? For God's sake, what the hell I am doing here? You have no right to do this!' Elijah shouted. Then he had a thought. 'Listen, I'll pay you double what you were promised if you let me go. Better still, I won't tell anyone about what has happened. Double the money. In cash. What do you say?'

The man considered the proposal for a second then he threw his head back and laughed.

'No, that won't work. You see, I was told that you have been a rather nasty little man. My employer thinks you should suffer, and I am paid to make you uncomfortable. Plus, it agrees with my ideals. See, I believe in justice. If a man does wrong, he needs to take responsibility for his own actions. Karma type of thing. My employer thinks you won't do that unless you're forced to. So he employed me. And, anyway, I don't think it will be you who pays me, will it? From what I've seen, you haven't much to offer me. But your ex-wife... well, that's a different story. Quite well off, I hear.'

He waggled his eyebrows in amusement, then leaned forward again and slapped his thigh with a dismissive hand.

'I must admit, mate, that I think you offering me your wife's money without her permission is wrong. You could have offered to have earned my respect or to work with me for the greater good, something like that, but instead you offer to steal someone else's money as a bribe. That is not good in my book. In fact, it's cowardly.'

Elijah tilted his chin in defiance. 'You gave the impression you would do anything for money,' he replied. 'I simply treated you with the disrespect that you deserve.'

The man suddenly shot forward, and his fist connected with Elijah's jaw. The tin cup rolled onto the floor, the hot liquid scalding Elijah's hand as he attempted to stand back up.

'Forget dinner. Make yourself comfortable.' As the man spoke, he walked over to the hatch they had entered, and twisted the iron wheel so that it sealed. Then he retrieved his head torch, fitted it onto his head, and switched it on.

Elijah realised too late what was happening. 'No, please don't leave me. Not here!'

But it was too late. The other hatch door had been opened and sealed shut. The electricity was switched off, and Elijah was left alone in complete darkness.

Chapter Twelve

The corridor was packed with people, most of whom Hammond didn't recognise, but he guessed they were members of various search teams. They were milling around, quietly chatting amongst themselves as Hammond passed them and entered the debriefing room. An older man in his late fifties stood by the window, creating a slim silhouette. He did not acknowledge Hammond as he entered, but stood isolated from the rest of the team seated around the table.

Edwards winked as Hammond shot him a questioning glance, as if to suggest the man's identity was something they were not privy to know. The man offered a discreet nod to Superintendent Morris when he entered the room, but otherwise remained anonymous and distant.

'We are treating the disappearance of Elijah Johnson as an abduction,' Morris began. 'This means our priority is his safe and prompt return. His ex-wife and girlfriend have each been allocated a family liaison officer to ensure their safety, and to act as a mediator should any information come in. Our second priority is to identify the perpetrator. Detective Inspector Hammond, Detective Sergeants Edwards and Williams will be working to identify motive and to trace the sender of the hostile threats that were set to Elijah before he disappeared. Those who are not assisting in the search will be processing and validating any witness reports and incoming intelligence. From now on, any information that comes in has to be treated in the strictest of confidence, and should be approved by DI Hammond or myself before it is passed to any third parties.'

Morris addressed the room, his eyes scanning from Hammond to DS Williams, Edwards, and the few extras that had evidently been pulled from their current investigations. He looked pale and tired. He turned his attention to the large screen behind him as images were uploaded.

'The phone data from Elijah's phone has provided us with some insight, although it is unclear as to the relevance at this time. We know that he used his mobile as portable internet reference, and luckily for us there are some bookmarked pages that seem to be of recent interest. We are looking at the most recently saved pages. One bookmarked page is the forum Quora, which asks whether passenger lists can be accessed from previous flights. It has been suggested that it may be relevant to his work, but I am tempted to dispel this theory, simply because Elijah has access to numerous detailed references on English law. This search could have been done on impulse, suggesting it is not related to his work.

'Secondly, we have a missing persons' page from 2018 to 2019. This was bookmarked following a Google search conducted in February, but this page has been returned to several times, the last time being a few days before Elijah went missing.

'The third bookmarked page is a news article from December 2017, referring to an incident on a morning flight from Gatwick to Zagreb on 7th November, 2017. Several passengers staged a protest when they saw a prisoner handcuffed to an officer as he was being deported to Croatia. The disturbance resulted in the detained man being taken off the flight, causing the flight to be delayed by several hours.' Morris paused for breath as he surveyed the room.

'All bookmarked sites are related by similar dates and location, which strongly suggests that Elijah had been researching something that was not related to his work.'

Hammond spoke up. 'We found travel insurance letters and paperwork relating to the European Quizzing Championships for November 2017, held in Zagreb. It is possible he was on the same flight.' He briefly shared the conversation he had shared with Dominic at the library. 'We know that he stayed at the Panorama Hotel in November 2017 when he attended the European Quizzing Championship, and Dominic suggested that Elijah was contacting them. Would it be far-fetched to assume he was asking about guest lists from November, since he was also researching how to access passenger lists from the same trip?'

Morris considered but shook his head slightly. 'We can't assume anything; we must deal with facts. There is evidently a connection, but we can only wait for that. connection to reveal itself. I'm happy for you to find out what you can, but double-check everything. If we assume wrongly, we will create more delays.'

He turned his attention to the tech team members in the room. 'Have we had any luck accessing the data from the public computer that Elijah had been using at the library?'

The answer was given by a man identifying himself as Mike, who stood up and addressed the room with confidence. Various sites that had been visited using Elijah's account login were listed. Most were research vehicles for his work, but there were more searches for media news items relating to the same Turkish Airways flight on November 7th, 2017. The deportee's name had been mentioned in one article, and that name had been searched in prison records, but it looked as if those searches had not been concluded.

Morris digested the information silently then asked Mike to hand over all information to Hammond and Edwards for their attention. He then gestured to the man by the window.

'Since our main objective is to locate Elijah as quickly and as safely as possible, I have requested external expertise.' He did not introduce his guest, but opened the door and invited the people in the corridor to enter the room. Within seconds, the room was packed with search operatives and tactical police personnel.

The man by the window took Morris's place at the front of the room. He gazed at his audience with a dispassionate air, not introducing himself or explaining his involvement, but instead referred to a map that was now being shown on the screen.

He spoke with an authoritative but calm voice. 'We are going to assume that your missing person has been taken into a series of tunnels that may still be accessible. Since the surrounding areas are owned by the Ministry of Defence, I cannot share the data acquisitions that have been compiled in recent years, but I can tell you that some of the underground structures have not been explored for decades at least. The information that I share now will be partly based on the study of vegetation indices that could give a clearer idea of how many underground structures there are or their size.

'There are several disused underground bunkers which will be investigated by military personnel at their discretion, but there are areas that are no longer under their jurisdiction. If your man entered an opening here...' He circled the shelter by the canal and traced his finger westerly along the canal until it rested just above an area marked by a Second World War Sound Mirror, '...it is possible he is heading north-westerly, where there is an underground concrete storage bunker located one hundred feet below the ground surface. This connects to a tunnel that zig-zags through the countryside for about five to eight miles towards the Old RAF airfield at Lympne.'

He cleared his throat and turned to face his audience. 'It is not an easy route, but it was constructed for a very specific reason in the 1940s, and there is good chance that it has remained in good condition. However, I am reluctant to allow too many people through the tunnel. We don't know how much damage the tunnel incurred during the earthquake of 2007. It may be necessary for non-specialist search operatives to search for any surviving ventilation shafts that run along the course of the tunnel, with the consideration that specialist searchers can be lowered down into the tunnels at various points.'

The man turned away from the map entirely and stood before them all, clasping his hands together in front of him as he addressed them.

'This information is sensitive, therefore I have asked that everyone in this room signs a confidential agreement before they leave. This may seem rather dramatic, but you will be entering military training grounds and security measures must be respected.'

He thanked his audience for their attention and then allowed Morris to delegate the tasks.

*

The team had made a breakthrough. The Panorama Hotel confirmed that Elijah had been making enquiries about previous hotel guest lists from November 2017. It was more difficult to access the airways data, but there was enough to believe they were being propelled on the right track.

'It must be related to the news article,' DS Williams muttered from his usual position peering at his computer screen. 'It is the only common denominator.'

He addressed Hammond. 'There were fourteen English competitors in the 2017 Quizzing Championships that year, plus seven other participants, such as those covering the media stories or who went as spectators. Elijah was not named as a competitor so we can assume he was there as a spectator. The hotel guest list has twelve names of English competitors staying at the hotel at the same time as Elijah. They were booked in from 3pm on the 7th November until the morning of the 12th November. Presumably, they travelled together from Gatwick on the same flight and witnessed the altercation that took place on the plane. I've compared the names with the missing persons' list that Elijah had compiled. Two names tallied. Two guests from the same hotel, staying at the same time, and presumably had travelled on the same flight, have been reported missing within a four-month period.'

Hammond raised his eyebrows and instantly peered at the screen Williams was referring to.

'It can't be a coincidence,' he said. He called over to Edwards who was sitting at his desk, deep in concentration at his own computer. 'What was the name of the man being deported on the flight to Zagreb?'

Edwards sauntered over to where they were standing, peering at his notes. 'Petar Hovat. He was twenty-two years of age at the time. According to reports, he had been taken directly to the plane from a security car on the forecourt, and had been shouting that he was being forcibly removed from his children. The passengers had responded in his defence, causing Home Office Officials to abandon the deportation attempt and return him to British custody.'

'What happened to him afterwards?'

Edwards shrugged. 'That is what I am trying to find out, but I'm not having much luck. From what I can tell, he is not on the prison system and doesn't appear to have been deported, but I'm chasing up on it now.' He offered a sardonic smile. 'You didn't ask me what had happened to him before the deportation attempt.'

Hammond shifted his weight off William's desk and attempted to stand straight, but had to bend again when his hip clicked. He grimaced and rubbed the area before realising it must look odd, so stood awkwardly whilst Edwards elaborated.

'Petar Hovat, a Croatian national, had been arrested and subsequently charged with the abduction and assault of a fourteen-year-old boy. When he was arrested, he was found in the act of planning another abduction of a minor. The charges were so serious he was deemed to be a serious threat to society, hence he was to be deported.'

DS Williams sighed heavily. 'And he had children. Jeez.'

'No, he didn't have any family in the UK,' Edwards clarified. 'That was said to gain the sympathy of the other passengers.'

'So, if the passengers prevented this man from being deported, effectively he was allowed back onto British soil whilst the justice system decided what to do next?' Hammond posed.

'So, it is logical to presume that Elijah and the two other missing people that were possibly on the same flight were three of the passengers who prevented Hovat's deportation.'

Hammond studied Williams. The man had a point. 'We need to dig deeper,' he said. 'We need to compare the information on the missing people that Elijah researched. If there is a link like you suppose, we may end up resolving three disappearances rather than one.'

*

'Hitler,' DS Williams announced suddenly that afternoon. He looked up, his half-chewed sandwich bulging in his cheek, as he called over to where Hammond had been inspecting the dregs of his coffee.

'Sorry?' Hammond looked up, startled out of his reverie. 'Did you say Hitler?'

DS Williams swallowed his mouthful and sauntered over to Hammond. 'You were talking about what Dominic had said in the library. Well, it's possible that when you asked him about tunnels in Hythe, he was associating. You said he spoke of a German plane heading to Lympne Airfield that had been allowed to land during war time? Well, that defence guy, or whatever he was, spoke about a tunnel that had been constructed for a specific purpose in the 1940s. It must be related to the attempted abduction of Hitler in 1941.'

Hammond tried to remember; there was a time when he had been fascinated by war stories.

'I thought it was Hitler who plotted to abduct the Pope and the Duke of Windsor?'

'No. Apparently some papers were unearthed by a military historian researching at the National Archives at Kew. There had been a tip-off that Hans Baur, a General in the Secret Service and Hitler's most trusted pilot, wanted to defect. The British devised a plan to allow Baur to fly Hitler to the airfield at Lympne, where they would then abduct him and take him to London for interrogation.'

Williams paused and ushered Hammond over to his computer. 'However, that was the story that was released. But I've found other rumours that British Intelligence had no intention of taking him to London, and that was what they proposed to Baur to ensure his compliance.'

Williams leant over his desk as he read from the screen before him.

'The story is that a Bulgarian called Kiroff had walked into the British Military Attaché's office in Sofia, telling them that his father-in-law, Baur, wanted to turn. But before then, the British had got wind of Nazi Germany's intention to invade the Western Soviet Union. They wanted to use the Soviet people as slave labour, acquiring their oil reserves, annihilate the Slavic people and repopulate it with Germans. So, when the British heard about Baur, it was too good an opportunity to use him to abduct Hitler and turn him over to the Russians.'

Hammond listened, giving silent nods to encourage his colleague to continue.

'There is evidence that three thousand extra men and weaponry were brought to Lympne to prepare for the arrival. There were urgent plans to construct a tunnel that led from the airfield to the coast, where Hitler was to be taken to a submarine in the English Channel and handed over to the Russians.'

Edwards spoke up. 'Well, we know it didn't happen, because the Germans invaded Russia later that year.'

'Well, obviously Baur didn't stick to the plan, but the British were convinced enough that it was going to happen, hence their preparations.'

'And you think that this was the tunnel that was mentioned in the briefing earlier?'

'Bound to be.'

Hammond scratched his head. 'I guess that is what Dominic was referring to. But how did he know? Evidently, it was not public knowledge, especially if the archived intelligence was limited. Do you think Elijah had told him about it? If he didn't, then how?'

'The same way I've found out; researching the area and cross-referencing. Or he could have a connection in the Military.'

'But we are still left with too many questions. Firstly, how did the abductor know about the tunnel? Do they have a military background? Or had Elijah gone to the tunnel voluntarily, either as a means to escape or taking someone there? Next question, why are they heading to Lympne Airfield? It's disused, and nothing but a conservation area now.'

'We need to think simply,' Edwards suggested. 'Elijah may have been writing quiz questions on that area and this information came up during his research.'

'In which case, the abductor is either local or is known to Elijah to have learnt that information, or they have military or ecological interests.' Hammond shook his head. 'There are too many possibilities, none of which we have time to validate.' He stood up straight and adopted a confident stance. 'Maybe the ex-wife or girlfriend will know.'

He directed his next question to DS Williams. 'Have you discovered anything about the two missing persons that had gone to Zagreb around the same time as Elijah?'

Williams nodded enthusiastically. 'There are two names that I'm looking at. One is Patricia Jenkins, aged thirty-seven. She disappeared from her apartment in Caterham in November 2018. I managed to trace her sister, who was willing to talk to me. She didn't have any idea whether Patricia had received threats before she went missing, but she did confirm that she had been a passenger on the same Turkish Airways flight to Zagreb as Elijah. She knew that Patricia had been involved in the protest against the man being deported. Apparently, the sister received a phone call just after Patricia had landed in Croatia, explaining why the flight had been delayed.

'The next person on Elijah's list was David O'Neal, aged fifty-five. He is an Engineer Production Manager working for EMT Plastics. He left his office to get the 18.21 train from London Bridge to Crawley in August 2018, and hasn't been seen since. There were no sightings of him at London Bridge or on the train, so it was assumed he disappeared somewhere between his office near Weston Street and London Bridge Station. His disappearance was treated as suspicious and is still being treated as a potential crime, because there had been threats made against him. However, it had been assumed by Mr O'Neal that the emails had been from his ex-wife, even though she denied it when questioned. The police investigation is ongoing.'

'Had he been a passenger on the same flight?'

'Yes. He had gone to Zagreb for work. There had been a baggage sticker on his suitcase that showed the same flight number. It was the last flight he had taken before his disappearance.'

For the first time that day, Hammond smiled. He was beginning to feel they were making a breakthrough.

CHAPTER THIRTEEN

The journey to Mischa Taylor's house near Mersham was only fourteen miles away from the station, so Hammond used the twenty-minute drive to summarise the progress the team had made. He was feeling hopeful. There was a good chance they had identified a possible motive for targeting Elijah, but the chances of the perpetrator being local was lessened by the possibility that they had targeted several other victims within an eighty-mile radius. It was a worrying realisation, because it meant the search for a possible abductor was nationwide.

There was no clue as to the perpetrator's identity, or even evidence that the sender of the threatening emails was the same person. Their entire investigation was based on presumption, but it was a presumption that had been formed by correlations, which was enough to satisfy Hammond for the time being. There was a chance that not all the questions would be answered, but if Elijah was found unharmed, that would be a positive outcome even if there was no absolute resolution.

Edwards had remained at the station to investigate the outcome of the failed deportation of Petar Hovat. It was surprising how difficult it was to find relevant information of past cases on the police mainframe. Hammond wished it was more like a television police drama, where all it took was a few clicks on a computer keyboard and suddenly every detail became apparent and the investigation was solved. The reality was far more frustrating, investigations more time consuming, and too many remained unsolved. Hammond's greatest fear was that Elijah would remain missing.

He took two wrong turnings before he found the road where Mischa Taylor's house was situated. It was on a quiet lane surrounded by fields, shadowed by the rolling North Downs above. It would be a nice place to retire to if the house prices were not too expensive. As Hammond parked near the entrance to the primary school around the corner from Mischa's house, he allowed himself to daydream for a moment. It would be convenient place to live if his grandchild attended the school nearby. He could collect his grandson or granddaughter, take them home for tea and quality time after school from time to time, or they could play a ball game in the field at the back.

A dog walker brushed against the car as they passed, startling Hammond out of his fantasy, and as he got out of the car he became aware of a cuckoo's call in the distance. For an inexplicable reason, it gave him a sense of *joie de vivre*. A few cars passed him as he walked down the road searching the names of the houses until he found Mischa's cottage, situated between a larger house and a row of garages.

The front garden was small but well tended. Trails of honeysuckle brushed him as he made his way up the narrow path to her front door. He heard Charlie barking before the door opened, and he crouched ready to welcome the small dog as it came out on the porch, stroking its head in greeting. He wondered how much the dog understood. As Hammond stood up, he met

Mischa's eyes and realised she had been crying recently. She had applied excessive mascara in an attempt to cover up her swollen eyelids, but her body language belied her emotional state. Her shoulders were slumped slightly, and as she shook Hammond's hand in greeting, her hand shook.

He followed her into the hallway and couldn't help but admire the numerous painted landscapes that were exhibited in a row as a corridor gallery advancing towards the kitchen at the back of the house. He peered closer at the artworks, and thought he recognised them as Constables, but refrained from asking. Mischa indicated he could wait in the small living room that overlooked the neighbour's garden, separated by a low privet. The room was small but beautifully furnished, with a tall rosewood bookcase and Victorian library table. He paused, debating where to sit, then arranged himself in a button-backed lounge chair nearest the window.

A flock of starlings was congregating outside, and Hammond watched them in fascination as Mischa bustled in the kitchen preparing drinks. As she re-entered the living room carrying a small tray, she affected a smile that didn't meet her eyes. It gave him the impression she wanted their meeting to be as quick as was reasonably polite.

'I have been updated.' Mischa handed Hammond a cup of tea with a floral design similar to the mugs he had seen in Elijah's kitchen. 'I appreciate the thought, but I don't think it is necessary for me to have regular visits by the liaison officer.'

Hammond thanked her for the drink and sipped the mint tea tentatively. Not enjoying the taste at all, he carefully placed the cup beside him on the nest tables.

'I realise it can feel intrusive,' he said, 'but there is a chance that Elijah is being coerced somehow, and if that is the case, you may be what they are using as bait.'

Mischa shook her head. 'No. I haven't been threatened. There haven't been any prowlers, nor have I had any sense that I am being watched. I don't think I am at risk. To be honest, I just want to continue my days as normally as possible.'

'Since you identified Elijah's phone, search teams have been deployed to check the area where it was found,' Hammond told her. 'It's a large area so it may take a while, but it will be thorough and you will be told as soon as there are any updates. In the meantime, I wanted to ask you if you knew what Elijah had been researching recently. Had he shared any of his work with you?'

Mischa raised her eyebrows. 'Such as?'

Hammond opened his hands in an innocent manner. 'Like local history? Had he shared anything that he had learnt about Hythe Canal or The Roughs, or anywhere local?'

'No. Elijah doesn't share his work with me. If I'm honest, trivia bores me.'

'Maybe you remember if Elijah shared his knowledge of the local landscape when you walked Charlie together sometimes?'

Mischa shook her head.

'What about his travels in the past? For example, the European Quizzing Championships in 2017?'

Mischa studied Hammond with a neutral expression for a prolonged moment. Hammond almost felt unnerved; he could not read her body language at all.

'I know he went, but it was before he and I became a

couple so I can't tell you anything about it,' she replied eventually. 'Like I said, quizzes bore me. I have no interest in them so there would be no reason for him to share anything like that.'

There was an awkward pause and Hammond sipped at his tea again, trying not to taste the liquid before he swallowed. 'You have a lovely home,' he said, and nodded towards the blue velvet sofa. 'That's a very unusual chair. I don't think I have ever seen one like it.'

Mischa looked down at and stroked the chair almost lovingly. 'This is a nineteenth century conversation seat,' she said. 'It was designed so that two people could face each other whilst they reclined in comfort.'

'It's very beautiful.' Hammond gazed around the room, taking in his surroundings with an appreciative eye. He noted that all around him there were objects of beauty and history. There was a glass door cabinet displaying antique tools, some of which Hammond couldn't identify, although he recognised a brass graphometer and several antique compasses.

Mischa followed his gaze. 'Some of those belonged to my husband,' she explained. 'He collected antique tools such as those, and gifted me some from his collection.'

Hammond twisted his body so that he could lean over the back of his chair, intrigued by the display. 'That has pride of place?' He smiled and pointed to an item made of brass, with a telescope and spirit level mounted on a tripod.

'That one has always my favourite although I don't really understand what it was used for. I've considered it a beautiful apparatus; the brass fittings and design are incredibly intricate.'

Hammond strained his eyes to examine the item. 'Is it a type of theodolite maybe?'

He was intrigued enough to look more closely and admire the other instruments, but became aware of Mischa standing up from her chair and arranging cups back onto the tray. He had the feeling that he had out-stayed his welcome.

Charlie wagged his tail a little as Hammond bade him goodbye, promising him a biscuit the next time they met. Mischa offered a half-hearted smile, but closed the door quickly as he left.

It's odd, Hammond thought, *it is as if she sees me as the enemy now.*

*

'I'm on my way there now,' Hammond confirmed to Edwards, when his colleague asked if he had seen Susan Maxwell.

'The tech guys have accessed Elijah's emails. Two messages have been sent since he went missing. At first, we were encouraged that Elijah had sent them, but it is now apparent that they were sent by Susan to the anonymous sender of the threatening emails.'

'Why?' The idea was ludicrous. Why would Susan behave in such a reckless manner when her ex-husband could possibly be in harm's way? 'How did she get access?'

'That is what I hoped you would find out, but that's not all.' Edwards paused. 'She offered money, a lot of cash, if they returned Elijah unharmed.'

Hammond slapped the car steering wheel and pulled over to a lay-by. He was trembling; the adrenaline was coursing him with the realisation that such an action could have severe repercussions to their investigation, as well as to the safety of Elijah.

'She's treating his disappearance as a kidnap!' Hammond uttered several expletives then recovered to ask, 'Did anyone reply?'

'No, to neither of the messages she sent. She sent the first message on the 13th, Saturday, and again yesterday.'

'Was this before or after we spoke to her yesterday?'

'After, about 4pm.'

'I'll talk to her. But it was definitely Susan who sent the messages? Mischa has access to his account.'

'She didn't sign the message, but she referred to Elijah as her ex-husband, which is enough.'

'I'll be there in ten minutes,' Hammond said. The car wheels spun as he exited the lay-by, his frustration evident as gravel scattered over the road behind him.

*

Hammond held his breath; the front door to Susan Maxwell's house was open. He paused at the door and called, but there was no response. He waited for a minute with an increasing sense of unease, then carefully entered the open door and instinctively followed the hallway into the reception room where he had recently sat with Susan.

It is generally assumed that death cannot be smelt by the human nose, but if the question was asked of any police officer or pathologist, they would agree that even a very recent death could be smelt strongly. It has a sickly sweet, almost coppery aroma that alerted Hammond to the fact that the woman lying on the sofa before him was, without doubt, lifeless.

Susan lay on her side on the sofa, both feet neatly placed on the cushions as if she had been laid to rest in a careful, almost loving manner. Her eyes were closed. Were it not for the dark stain on her otherwise light silver hair, she could be asleep.

He moved carefully into the room and approached Susan, feeling her neck for a pulse, hoping there would be a sign of life. But there was none. He knew he had to call someone, but for a moment he hesitated and stood in the same spot, gazing around the room noting details that may or not be relevant. Only a few minutes earlier, he had felt such frustration and anger towards this woman. Now he just felt sadness.

He walked back outside and phoned the station.

CHAPTER FOURTEEN

'It doesn't make sense.' Hammond was outside the house. He hunched his shoulders, digging his hands deeper into his jacket pockets as a chill descended around him. A burp of mint tea threatened to escape, but he covered it by talking quickly. 'It couldn't have been done deliberately, surely? The comfortable positioning of the body is almost an act of care.'

Edwards scoffed, 'After bashing her brains in?' He shook his head and the two men watched as the crime scene technicians began processing the scene.

'The neighbours didn't see or hear anything. It certainly gives the impression that she was hurt by someone she knew.' Hammond sighed. He ran his hand over his face, as if placing an imaginary shield of calm around him. 'This is madness. When will this ever stop?'

Edwards glanced sideways at him. 'It's just getting to you,' he said. 'It happens to us all, but you know by tomorrow it will all seem normal.'

'That's just it. Discovering new ways in which people hurt one another is part of our every day. Our sense of normality is warped.'

Edwards offered a sympathetic slap on Hammond's back. 'You'll miss it when you retire, though.'

Hammond smiled at the irony. Despite the fact that he had been counting the days to starting a new life in retirement, he still wondered what he would do with his days. He left Edwards to confer with the officers cordoning off the driveway.

Dr Ed Henderson removed his glasses when he saw Hammond. 'It looks like a simple blow to the head.'

'Is there a way of knowing what caused the injury?' Hammond covered his mouth just in time before another burp escaped. He grimaced, repelling the taste of the mint tea that insisted on repeating itself.

Henderson ignored the belch and shook his head. 'Nothing that I can see here. It's possible the assailant took the weapon with them. But judging from the spots of blood residue on the rug and sofa, the victim was moved onto the sofa whilst she was alive. She would have been disorientated but possibly conscious. I'll know more when I examine her properly, but I will hazard a guess this was not a murder attempt – possibly an argument that got heated and resulted in violence. It looks like there were attempts to resuscitate her. There's very slight bruising and pressure marks on both sides of the jaw, as if her head had been held, and pressure marks on the mouth and slight bruising on the chest. I'm guessing it won't be too difficult to find traces of the other person.'

'Unless someone else discovered Susan after the attack and tried to resuscitate her?' Hammond suggested.

'It would have been very soon after death. I don't think she has been dead longer than four hours. You've been here about an hour now?' Henderson motioned that he had completed his initial examination, and walked with Hammond back to the entrance driveway.

'I've already been briefed by your Superintendent,' he said. 'I know this is seen to be part of an ongoing investigation, so I will aim to have a report for you first thing in the morning.'

*

By 7pm the skies were dark with the threat of imminent rain. Hammond parked the car closest to the police station, noting that Edwards' car had arrived there already. He took the stairs two at a time, but regretted it when he opened the door and wheezed an indecipherable greeting to his colleagues.

'I didn't think you would be here.' It was unusual for Edwards to work too late in the evenings.

'I wanted to update you on the whereabouts of Petar Hovat.' Edwards shrugged in a casual manner as he answered, but it was obvious he was avoiding having to explain why he wasn't heading home at the first opportunity.

'Hovat was eventually deported back to Croatia earlier this year,' he explained, 'but before that he was temporarily held at Belmarsh from February 2018. After the first failed attempt at deporting Hovat, he was fitted with an electronic tag and released on bail. Within the day, an alert was generated at the monitoring centre that Hovat had left his curfew address, but it took several hours to find him, during which time he had abducted a boy delivering pizza and refused to tell authorities where he had left him.'

'But surely Hovat's movements were tracked?'

'Yes, but you know as well as I do that tagging is only effective once the defendant has left the house. In this case, the boy delivered to the curfew address, where he was attacked and then taken to his own burial site some time later.'

Hammond sighed. 'Oh God. So Hovat killed him. Do you know how?'

Edwards nodded. 'The post mortem examination concluded that he had been drugged and physically abused, but it was the combination of hypnotic sedatives and recreational drugs that killed him.'

Hammond shook his head angrily. 'How the hell could it have happened? Although as far as our investigation is concerned, that is a heck of a motive. By preventing Hovat from leaving the UK, the protesters on the plane unwittingly contributed to the later events.' He retrieved his notes. '*You deserve to suffer the way you made us suffer,*' he read aloud. 'Does that mean that the vendetta is being actioned by more than one person?'

He threw the notebook back on the desk and faced Edwards. 'Any news on the search?'

Edwards shook his head. 'I haven't been told details. There have been possible findings that indicate the tunnel has been entered recently, but I haven't been privy to all the information yet.'

Hammond nodded and allowed a slow exhale of breath whilst he considered the next course of action. He was aware he had not breathed properly for a while. The stress had caused him to act and think fast, and events had been spiralling too quickly for him to take a moment and reflect.

'There's not much we can do tonight, not until we get the initial post mortem results for Susan Maxwell. Tomorrow, I want to find out all the details relating to the murdered pizza delivery boy. There may be a name that we can link to the disappearances.' His voice trailed off, realising that the next day would be the seventh day since Elijah had gone missing. A whole week had gone by, and they still had no idea what had happened to him.

*

When Hammond got home to his flat in Folkestone, it was past eight o'clock. Paul sat on the sofa, the light from his mobile phone beaming upwards in the otherwise darkened room, illuminating his features like a hollowed-out skeletal mask. He was dressed in jeans and a hooded jumper, and looked a lot younger than a man in his thirties.

Forgiving the grunt that came in reply to his greeting, Paul was evidently engrossed in the football game app that he was playing, Hammond went into the bathroom and took a long shower, standing under the torrent of water as if expecting it would wash the cause of his unease away. Then, putting on his bathrobe, he went into the kitchen and scanned the fridge, hoping it would offer a surprise. It didn't. Half a stalk of broccoli, leeks, an un-opened bag of carrots, half a can of cannelloni beans, milk, and a block of cheddar. There were some remnants of cream cheese past its use-by date, but not enough to cover a cracker. He needed to go shopping again. He hadn't anticipated how quickly food would disappear when Paul was at home.

There was a bottle of ruby ale on the bottom fridge door shelf, which he selected as compensation, and returned to the living room where he sat opposite Paul and sipped at the beer from the bottle.

'Have you made a decision yet?' he asked over the rim of the bottle.

Paul answered without raising his eyes. 'Yes.'

'Ah.'

Paul didn't elaborate, so Hammond continued to sip slowly waiting for his son to look up and continue the conversation. Minutes passed silently until eventually Hammond plunged in.

'I've been thinking about becoming a grandfather,' he said.

Paul looked up, met his father's eyes, and raised an eyebrow.

'I like the idea,' Hammond went on. 'In fact, I like the thought of having a grandchild more than I expected to. But here's the thing...' He shuffled his weight towards the front of the chair, his bathrobe slipping down at the sides of his legs, revealing his naked thighs. He tucked the robe in the middle of his lap and looked at Paul with a serious expression.

'I love you and I love Jenny,' he went on, 'but I must admit that I think if you were to be the father of her child, you would be short-changing yourself. I am sure she would make a great, if eccentric, mother, and you two would undoubtedly make wonderful choices for the benefit of the child. But if I am honest, I want to see you emotionally fulfilled, to have a child with a woman you love and who loves you as a partner, not just as a best friend. If I could share with you the joy your mother and I felt when you were born and how happy we were raising you as co-parents, that is what I want you to experience, too.'

'But you and Mum divorced.'

Hammond waved a hand, dismissing the point. 'But we were married eighteen years, and those years were wonderful. We saw you develop into a fine young man, and we couldn't be prouder of each other or of you.'

Paul studied his father until a faint smile developed across his face.

'You're a soft bastard,' he said, but his tone was gently appreciative. He resumed his football game and, without looking up, added, 'I agree. I made the same decision myself. In fact, when I woke up, I told Bettina I wanted a divorce, and then this afternoon I signed up to a dating agency.'

The sudden gulp of beer caused it to splutter over Hammond's chin as he choked with delight.

CHAPTER FIFTEEN

'It is likely that the sudden deceleration caused the brain to hit the skull twice. The impact caused the brain to ricochet off the skull wall before hitting it again at such force that it tore the nerve fibres. She wouldn't have been conscious for very long.'

'So, it could have been accidental?'

'Yes, if she had been pushed backwards onto a hard edge, but there was nothing in the room with any evidence of an impact. No biological residue on any of the examined furniture edges.'

Hammond wanted clarification, but felt he was not getting a definitive answer. Attempting to mask his irritation, he tried another tactic.

'So, from your examination of the wound, if something had been used as a weapon and hit Susan on the back of the head, would it have caused the same effect than if she had accidentally fallen backwards and hit her head on a static object?'

'Yes, in theory. It is dependent on the force of deceleration and subsequent impact. But if she had been pushed, there would be a pressure mark on her body from the hand that pushed her, and there is no evidence of that. Also, the angle of the wound would normally give indication as to whether the blow was from above or from below, but in this instance it is inconclusive.'

Hammond frowned. 'So, in other words, you cannot confirm if the death was accidental or deliberate.'

'Exactly,' Henderson replied. 'But I can confirm that there was someone else in direct contact with the deceased immediately after the impact, if not during. I have found a foreign hair and saliva on the lips, which shouldn't take too long to identify if you get comparison samples.'

Hammond thanked Henderson half-heartedly but was stopped from ending the call as Henderson interjected quickly. 'Oh, one more thing. This may be relevant, but there was a slight hint of fragrance, like male cologne, on the victim's clothing. It was around her chest area.'

'Is there a way of testing it?'

Henderson whistled down the phone line as he considered. 'Unlikely, because it isn't like make-up. If it was foundation or lipstick, for example, it would be possible to identify the brand, but when fragrance is found on clothing it is not so easy. For a start, it depends not only on the method of transference but the persistence qualities. Susan's shirt was 100% cotton, but I assume that it came into contact with the other person's clothing, which had previously absorbed an odorant. The identification of the components won't be possible as they're not at high enough concentrations.'

'But you have an idea it is a male aftershave or something similar?' Hammond pressed.

'Yes, but I'm not swearing by it. My theory is that if the other person had rested their head on Susan's chest, listening for a heartbeat for example, traces of their cologne had transferred onto her clothing.'

Hammond ended the call and tried to decide if the information just given by the pathologist was helpful. He didn't know where to start.

Susan had not been in a relationship at the time of her death, so it was less likely that the attempted revival had been by a lover, especially since no-one had come forward to give information or with enquiries.

If Susan had been insurance used to encourage Elijah to comply with his abductor's instructions, why would they harm her? Unless Elijah had managed to escape and they had fulfilled their threat? But if so, what would they gain as a result? Elijah wouldn't come running back to them, unless he also feared for Mischa.

Another consideration could be that the abductor had been aggravated by Susan's offer of money and had struck in anger. But what would be their reason, and why would they have gone to see Susan in the first place?

It didn't make sense. He said so to Edwards.

'It shouldn't be too hard to figure out,' his colleague replied. 'Think about it. You were angry when you heard that Susan had offered money to the possible abductor, so it makes sense that someone else was angry for the same reason. Especially if it is your partner's ex-wife interfering in such a way that she is not only endangering Elijah but acting as if she is his principal point of call. There could be jealousy at play here.'

Hammond nodded. It would make sense. 'You mean Mischa? But I saw her at her house that afternoon, and she did not give the impression of having just arrived back home.'

Edwards raised a shoulder. 'How long does it take to drive from her house to Susan Maxwell's? Twenty minutes? It's possible.'

Hammond nodded and phoned Henderson; his conversation was brief but non-conclusive. No dog hairs had been found at the scene or on the body.

'Still, it's worth questioning her.'

*

Hammond's stomach was rumbling loudly. He rummaged in the desk drawer looking for a snack. He was sure he had left a cereal bar in there a week or so ago. Not finding anything, he massaged his stomach and considered how to fill it, but was interrupted in his considerations when Edwards came in.

'There's been an update from the search in the tunnel. There's been definite recent activity and there appear to be two sets of footprints. A battery from a head torch has been found, and it seems it was dropped very recently. It's being processed now and we're due to have an update within the next two hours. I may head over there but am waiting for confirmation first.'

Hammond nodded but felt despondent. 'I'd be more enthusiastic if they had actually found him. It feels as if we are simply following a trail of breadcrumbs.'

Edwards took up a defensive stance, placing his hands on his hips. 'So, what do you propose we do that we aren't doing already?'

Hammond shrugged. He ran his hand through his hair and studied his desk for a prolonged moment. 'I'm due to interview Mischa, but I want to wait for the DNA samples to be compared with any data we have first.' He stood up. 'I need to eat and think.'

He asked Edwards to phone with any incoming news, and left the station in search for nourishment.

*

Hammond didn't intend to walk into town, but once he had inhaled the fresh air, he felt energised and decided to prolong the walk. He stopped at a vegetarian whole-foods cafe, normally a place he would have avoided, but the aroma of freshly baked cheese scones was too entic-ing. He sat at a small table just inside the door and watched the world pass by outside. It was tempting to sit there for the rest of the day and forget all the stresses of police work.

Morris's offer to let him go early had been tempting, and there had been moments when Hammond had wanted to walk out of the office and not return. This was such a moment. He was becoming exhausted by the extremes of hope and despair that seemed to constantly fluctuate without any sign of normalising. One minute he felt they were making a breakthrough, the next he was convinced there would no resolution. Maybe they would never know what had happened to Elijah. He wouldn't be the first to disappear without a trace, but that gave Hammond more reason not to give up. He couldn't leave his career without closure.

The cheese scone was still warm, and the butter melted as soon as it was spread. The food comforted him and allowed him to relax. Hammond was aware that he hadn't been feeling well, but he didn't know what the problem was. It wouldn't be something that he could clarify if he consulted a doctor. Not feeling well could imply so many things, yet deep down, Hammond was concerned. He was not a hypochondriac. On the contrary, he could be described as a man who usually took his health for granted. But lately he had found himself worrying about whether he should update his will, or what he would decide if he were given a choice of life-prolonging treatment or dismissing medical intervention and settling for a quicker death. The thoughts were random and had no basis, but the constant headaches, fatigue, and frequent bouts of nausea were becoming too obvious.

His mobile was ringing. The voice on the other end was impatient and curt.

'I need you here now.'

Hammond left the remainder of his scone and jogged back to the station.

*

Superintendent Morris was on the phone and indicated that Hammond should sit and wait whilst he ended the call. He rummaged for a pen, jotted notes on a Post-It, and stuck the note on his computer screen before finally addressing Hammond.

'I wanted to share updates with you before we all meet this afternoon. There have been several findings that are indicating significant progress. There's no doubt that the tunnels have been used frequently; the old electrical wiring that was cut before the tunnels were blocked, has evidently been repaired. Fingerprints were taken from the new terminal blocks. A discarded AA battery had also been found earlier, further down the canal end of the tunnel. Again, a partial thumbprint was found. These prints have been processed and I've been advised that not only do both sets match, but they have identified a person of interest from the PND.'

Despite the positive news, Morris's face did not show encouragement. Instead, he leaned forward on the desk and clasped his hands together, as if he was about to impart bad news. Hammond waited, whilst his supervisor deliberated his next sentence.

He's about to take me off the case, Hammond thought, as he telepathically willed the man in front of him to speak. An image was forming in his imagination of leaving the office with a handshake, followed by a kick up the backside out the station's back door.

'What I am about to say has not been shared with the rest of the team,' Morris began, 'but it is inevitable that the information will be shared at some point, and I wanted to give you a chance to hear it beforehand.'

Hammond sat forward in anticipation, noting that Morris looked embarrassed.

'No doubt you remember, when you tragically lost your home in the fire years ago, we had to investigate the arson attack without your cooperation.'

Hammond nodded, confused. Nine years ago, Hammond had been the target of an arson attack that had destroyed his home in Stanford. Whilst he and Jenny, who had been staying with Hammond at the time, were recovering in hospital, the debris had been examined and the body of his former Chief Inspector had been found in the kitchen. There had been no explanation at the time, and it had been necessary for the Major Crime Directorate to investigate Hammond and Jenny as murder suspects.

Morris cleared his throat nervously before continuing. 'You may remember that, at the time, I mentioned to you that your son's friend had been investigated and we had found something notable on her background check.'

Hammond coughed. 'Yes, I vaguely recall you mentioning something.'

Morris looked down at his notes. 'The only reason I am mentioning this is because at the time you told me you didn't want to know, but it is relevant now.' He passed a piece of paper across the table to Hammond, who read what was in front of him.

'Ghost Orchid,' he read. 'I don't understand. They're a vigilante group?'

'Yes, and your friend Jenny was an active member with them. As far as we know, she was not suspected of having committed any crime, but one of the suspected founders of the group, Joshua Stadden, was often highlighted as a potential person of interest for his broadcasting of vigilantism. They are his fingerprints that we have found in the tunnel.'

Hammond read further. He was quiet whilst he studied the paperwork in front of him.

'He's been targeting migrants arriving on British shorelines?'

Morris leaned forward to retrieve the papers. 'Yes, that is his latest antic. He and several other members use a motorised dingy to patrol the shoreline around the Dymchurch coast, recording their activities on social media. Their latest posting was a video where they filmed themselves circling around an overcrowded boat of migrants, announcing their intention to cause the other boat to overturn and drown the passengers.'

'Jenny wouldn't be involved in that!' Hammond blustered his disbelief.

'No. I'm not suggesting she would. As far as I am aware, Jenny's name has not been involved with the group for a while now, but I just wanted you to be aware that she may be mentioned.'

Hammond thanked him for the consideration; he was quiet for a while before returning to senior officer mode.

'So, someone has been in the tunnel, but there is nothing to suggest that they are with Elijah? Or was there more?' he asked.

Morris nodded. 'Yes. Elijah's prints were found at the scene. A complete handprint was found on the door of a connecting bunker on this area here.' He spread a local map on the table and pointed to a circle in red pen, north of Lympne Castle. 'We've localised the search to the area around the old airfield, so at least we can now concentrate on one area.'

Hammond deliberated, 'So, if we assume that Elijah is with this vigilante guy, do we have any clue as to their connection?'

Morris shook his head. 'None. There is nothing that we have seen in Elijah's background to suggest any links at all. But we are sure that we need to focus on Mr Stadden as our likely abductor. I'll send officers out to his known addresses and contacts, as priority. You need to find anything that can explain how and why a vigilante group would have a grudge against Elijah Johnson.'

Hammond blew out his cheeks, indicating the challenge. 'I need to interview Mischa Taylor.'

Morris nodded. 'As far as I am concerned, you have been debriefed, so there's no need to join us this afternoon for the team meeting, but let me know if anything comes up.'

'Do I mention Joshua Stadden to Mischa, in case it rings any bells?' he asked.

'I'll leave it to you,' Morris replied. 'I presume you are formally interviewing her regarding Susan's death?'

Hammond nodded.

His mind was buzzing. He was feeling a mixture of relief that Elijah had been traced, if not found, and even more so that they had an identified possible suspect. But he was dismayed by the information Morris had shared about Jenny. He wasn't her parent and she had not been his responsibility, but he had judged her to be a young woman with common sense and moral intelligence. To have her name associated with a group that was renowned for its ethnic profiling and vindictive actions, was something he couldn't tolerate.

He had wanted to phone her the second he had left Morris's office, but work had to come first, especially now they were getting closer to finding Elijah.

*

Mischa was clearly surprised to have been summoned to the station. She shot a resentful glance towards Hammond as she sat opposite him in the interview room, her posture hinting at defiance, with a straight back and chin held high. She did not return Hammond's pleasantries, even though he had offered reassurances that she was not being accused in any way, but stayed quiet until he had asked his first question.

'Can you tell me the last time you saw Susan Maxwell, Elijah's ex-wife?'

'Months ago, maybe even a year. It was a quick introduction.'

'Have you had any contact since, whether it is by telephone or email?'

'Yes, you know I have. Last Thursday morning, I phoned her asking if she knew where Elijah was.'

'Have you had any contact with her since?'

Mischa shook her head. 'I have had no reason to. I was told by the liaison officer who visited me that Susan was also being updated by Police.'

'When you were told of Susan's death, were you concerned for your own safety?'

Mischa studied her fingers before she looked up. 'Not at all.'

When asked to verify her movements during the time of Susan's death, she willingly shared details of a conversation she had had in her next-door neighbour's kitchen.

'They understand that I am feeling helpless, that I am so worried about Elijah. They were showing kindness by allowing me to rant over a coffee.'

'You are worried because you believe Elijah has been taken against his will?'

Mischa frowned. 'Yes! The emails that I showed you were threatening. You know this! Why are you asking me?'

Her pitch was heightening. Hammond looked at her sympathetically.

'Susan had sent emails to the sender of the hostile emails received by Elijah. She offered money to them in exchange for the safe return of Elijah. We know that this was not the first time that Susan offered large amounts of cash. Were you aware of this?'

Her tone lowered. 'No.'

'Elijah didn't tell you about the emails himself?'

'Like I said earlier, no, he didn't tell me about them. I found them after he disappeared.'

'Can you think of a reason why he would tell Susan and not you?'

Hammond's conscience told him he was being unkind by asking, but he needed to see a sign of jealousy that could substantiate Edward's theory.

Mischa leaned forward. 'No, I don't know why, but I didn't really understand their relationship. I guess he saw her as a mother figure whilst he regarded me more as a lover.'

Hammond controlled the upward twitch of his mouth and changed tack.

'Do you know the name Joshua Stadden?'

Mischa repeated the name and shook her head. 'No, why should I?'

The interview was brief. Hammond spoke to Mischa for no longer than twenty minutes. He left the interview room with instructions for her to leave a DNA sample for comparison. There was a sense of renewed vigour with the belief he was making progress.

CHAPTER SIXTEEN

Hammond's trouser pocket was vibrating; he retrieved his phone and read the text that had alerted him. The message was from Jenny.

We need to talk. I'll come to yours tonight. When will you be home?

He sent a quick message back before heading to the meeting room where Morris was completing his debrief with the rest of the team. He stood patiently by the door until Morris met him, and they sauntered back to the privacy of the Superintendent's office. Morris shut the door and listened with attention as Hammond gave an update on his meeting with Mischa.

'So, what is your feeling about her?' Morris asked when Hammond had paused.

Hammond leaned back in the chair and stretched his leg as he sought an itch under his trouser leg. He scratched while he answered.

'It's odd. I felt she was not as honest as I had previously perceived her to be. I can't put my finger on it, though, and evidently the woman is under a lot of strain, so it may not indicate anything...'

'But your instinct is telling you something is not right with her account?'

Hammond winced as he scratched too hard and pulled his trouser leg back down, realising he had caused himself to bleed.

'The first thing that struck me was when I asked her if she felt vulnerable following the suspicious death of Susan. Mischa wasn't just in denial that there was a chance she could be at risk, she was absolutely sure that she would not be hurt despite the circumstances of Elijah's disappearance. That's odd. She's tired, stressed, and desperately worried about her partner. Usually there's a tendency to be paranoid or overly-anxious, possibly even more open to suggestion, yet she was none of those. Her body language confused me.'

'How?'

Hammond sighed and opened his hands wide. 'I don't know, I may be overanalysing... Like I said, I can't put my finger on it, but her behaviour was contradictory to what she was saying at times.'

Morris leaned forward. 'It could be nothing or it could be something worth noting. You've always followed your instinct. What's your gut telling you?'

Hammond laughed. 'There was a time when you used to say I should follow facts rather than instinct. You've mellowed!' He paused, then went on, 'But, to be fair, I have no idea what my gut is telling me.' He sighed. 'It's strange. I dreaded retirement but now I realise I am not the detective I once was. I'm indecisive, I can't process facts the way I used to.'

Morris smiled. 'That's age, isn't it? We're constantly trying to keep up with the new methods or technology. Eventually the new and young take over and replace us.'

Hammond nodded. 'It's time to retire, I know it. My body knows it, but I need to find closure on this. At least allow me the opportunity to stay until there's a resolution.'

Morris stood up and retrieved his coffee cup from beside the filing cabinet, then walked to the door and indicated Hammond follow him. They wandered back up the corridor.

'There may not be a resolution,' he said, 'but I am happy to allow you to continue until we have some answers at least. Of course, it may be possible that the possible motive you discovered has nothing to do with Elijah's disappearance. He may be planning something with this vigilante group. Do you know if Elijah had any interest in any justice groups?'

'Nothing like that has been mentioned, nor has there been any evidence to suggest it. I'll learn more about this Ghost Orchid group, and hopefully we will uncover any leads there. Edwards hasn't found Stadden yet – he hasn't got a home address, but we will try his contacts.'

As Hammond walked off, he considered what Morris had said and realised what it was that had made him feel so unsure about Mischa. When he had asked if she had recognised Joshua Stadden, she did not shake her head or answer with a simple 'No'. She had paused and repeated the name before denying. In Hammond's experience that was a ploy to play for time whilst attempting to hide a true reaction. His instinct had been trying to warn him that Mischa did recognise the name of her partner's possible abductor. But how? And why did she deny it?

*

As promised, Hammond arrived outside his flat just after 5pm, but was surprised to see Jenny was already waiting outside the block of flats. Her hair had been cropped close to the ears, giving her a more impish appearance with her slim, short stature. Despite being in her early thirties, she looked not much older than a teenager.

He greeted her warmly, but she stopped him from advancing further into the building, and tilted her head to one of the upstairs buildings. 'Bettina is in there with Paul,' she said. 'Best we leave them for the time being.'

Hammond agreed a bit too enthusiastically, but he knew Jenny would understand his desire to avoid Bettina. They walked towards the harbour. Despite his genuine pleasure in seeing Jenny, there was a need within him to shout his frustration at her stupidity for her former involvement with a vigilante group. However, he restrained himself, and instead admired the harbour which was looking particularly picturesque with the sun glinting through hazy clouds.

'I am really peed off with you, Wally.' Jenny walked beside him with her hands hooked in the apron of her dungarees. 'In fact, I just want to yell at you. You have really hurt me.'

She looked up at him then, her eyes filling with moisture, her face taut with a tormented expression.

Hammond stopped walking and turned to face her. 'Why?' His surprise was genuine, his voice less distinctive from the high-pitched shrieks of the gulls circling above them.

Jenny opened her mouth wide as if she was struck dumb with disbelief then she hit him hard, her fist connecting with his waist. He stepped back and looked at her, demanding an explanation.

She turned her back on him and walked over to the harbour wall where she sat and drew her knees up to her chest, her head bowed. Hammond approached her, unsure what to do, but then sat beside her and allowed her the opportunity to vent.

'I thought you and I were like family,' she said, 'but now I hear that you do not consider me good enough to have your grandchild.'

'That's not it ...' Hammond began, but she continued as if he had not said anything.

'I thought that Paul and I could have something together that was special, that would mean something to us all, as a family. Bettina doesn't want children but Paul does, so it seemed the perfect solution. We could all have been a family without having to compromise on our ideals, other than yours evidently. But Paul has decided that not only does he not want to share parenting with me, he wants to leave his wife... all because you disagreed with his intentions.'

Hammond held up a hand in defence. 'No, that's not true. I just want Paul to be happy, and I think he needs a wife who cares for him rather than an overbearing brute of a pseudo-woman who leans so far to the right that she thinks bent.'

Jenny stared at him. 'Oh, my goodness, you really hate her.'

Hammond was quiet for a moment. 'I don't hate Bettina, Jenny, but I can't tolerate her either. I have absolutely no desire to be anywhere near the woman. She's no good for Paul.'

Jenny shouted at him, 'Who are you to say that? They were happy together before you even knew they were a couple! It seems to me that you are too biased against her. Yes, I agree she is different from the woman you would expect Paul to have fallen in love with, but in other ways, I admire her.'

Hammond allowed his laugh to escape. The idea of anyone having admiration for Bettina was farcical. 'How? She's insensitive and crass. I agree I haven't spent much time in her company, but on the rare occasions when I have been in her presence, not once have I heard her say anything considerate, affectionate, or even faintly amusing. All I have heard from her is repeated mantras of petty prejudices.'

Jenny stared at him, her jaw tense and eyes wide with anger. 'How many women do you know that have the confidence to be seen in their natural state, to resist conforming to the rules of gender identification? Bettina doesn't pretend to be anything other than herself, because she has the confidence to behave as she pleases. She doesn't care about having to behave or present herself in a certain way, to shave her legs, or dress to conform to certain standards or ideals. That has to be admired! How many people can do that?'

Hammond chuckled. 'Just knowing she doesn't shave her legs is enough to put me off!' He had meant it in a light-humoured way, but Jenny did not share the humour. She was almost enraged.

'Why? Do you shave your legs? Does anyone care? Why is it necessary for women to care about what people think, but you don't care if you don't shave your face every day. God, Wally! I always thought you were fair-minded, honest and kind, but now I see you differently.'

Hammond couldn't help himself. 'Ditto!' he spat the words as the suppressed frustration towards her suddenly found their outlet.

Jenny stopped shouting. She read his expression and was surprised by the anger in his expression.

'What are you implying?'

'Two words, Jenny...' Hammond got up from the wall and looked down at her. 'Ghost Orchid!'

Jenny stared at him for a few seconds, then she swallowed and quietly asked, 'What about them?'

'Why, Jenny? Why be involved with such a group of anarchists?'

She gazed towards the pier and sighed. 'Come on, Wally, let's get some chips.' She took his arm and the two of them headed towards the harbour. To anyone watching, they looked like a mismatched pair; the elf and the oaf heading off to tea.

The chips were deep fried to perfection, plump and salty, just the way Hammond liked them best. Jenny chomped on them with gusto, occasionally stopping to squirt lashes of ketchup before resuming her attack on the next fried potato. After a while, she turned her attention to him.

'We weren't anarchists,' she said. 'Not at the beginning, anyway. We shared a cause that we believed in; we were aiming for the greater good.'

'For what exactly?' Hammond finished his chips and screwed up the wrappings. He waved away the seagull that was pecking at anything resembling a crumb near their feet.

'For justice.'

'Surely that is the point of law enforcement,' Hammond interjected wryly.

'Yes, but sometimes the law can be too complex. It's not about right or wrong. It comes down to what can be proved, and in some cases, wrong-doing cannot be proven.'

'So explain.' Hammond sat back in the plastic chair and crossed his arms.

Jenny sighed. She had ketchup on her chin and she wiped it roughly away with the paper napkin before she answered.

'I haven't told you much about my childhood. There was no need, and despite you wanting to know, you always respected that I didn't want to share details, but twenty years ago I had a reason to distrust the police and the whole justice system. I had witnessed the guilty be protected by the law and their victims get stigmatised. It was an abuse of power; one that I wanted to reverse. When I was a student, I mentioned my anger to a classmate. I told him about my childhood experiences of an abusive father and an abused mother, and he introduced me to the group that had called themselves Ghost Orchids.'

'What was the name of this student friend?'

Jenny frowned. 'I can't remember. All I know is that the group was in its infancy; we were just a small, ideal-istic group of young people who felt we could make a difference to society by exposing those who did wrong, and make their crimes known so they couldn't hide behind bureaucracy.'

Hammond nodded. 'Some countries encourage such activity amongst their societies. The number of convic-tions for paedophiles has risen since citizens intervened in such cases. But Ghost Orchid earned a reputation for extremism. How were you involved?'

Jenny sat up straighter in her chair. 'I had nothing to do with any crimes committed. The sad fact is that some members were extremists with a grudge against anyone who gravitated from the norm. Whereas some were simply trying to help society by exposing wrong-doing, there were others who wanted to stigmatise or commit extortion. When that became obvious, I turned my back on them.'

'When was this exactly?' he asked.

Jenny cocked her head to one side whilst she tried to remember. 'I was about nineteen at the time when I was first introduced to them, so it must have been around 2005, but I left them about a year later. There was an incident where one of the members campaigned against a mentally disabled man accused of sexual harassment. Even though we discovered the accusation was unfounded, the accused man was violently attacked, and the abuse was videoed and shared on social media. I got scared when I realised that instead of finding such an attack repugnant, those responsible were applauded and encouraged to do more. It was sick.'

Hammond saw her shame was evident. 'But you were associated,' he told her. 'Your details were included in the police report.'

Jenny dismissed this with a vehement shake of her head. 'No. Absolutely not. I was simply there when the police turned up at the house and made arrests. They took my name. That was all. But I promise you, Wally, I had nothing to do with any of that. It disgusted me.'

'Did you know Joshua Stadden?'

'Not personally, but I know of him. He was one of the founders of the group apparently. But because the group was so secretive, we never knew people's real identities – not at first, anyway, and he didn't come to all the meetings so I didn't have much to do with him.'

Hammond smiled. He believed her and was relieved by the revelations. He stood up. 'Do you think they've finished at the flat yet?'

Jenny collected her chip wrappings and threw them in the bin as they passed. 'It shouldn't take them too long to kiss and make up. I hope Paul has seen sense and changes his mind about divorcing her.'

Hammond was silent. He daren't share his opinion, which was the exact opposite, but Jenny read his expression. 'I simply want Paul to be happy,' she said as explanation.

'Of course, just that I wonder if he can find happiness elsewhere. I'm sorry, Jenny, I just really believe Paul is better off counting his losses and starting again.'

Jenny stopped walking. She looked up at him and placed her hand on his arm. Her tone was gentle, but her eyes showed sincerity.

'Paul loves Bettina, you have to honour that. Do you remember when Paul was so angry at you when you and Lyn split up? He accused you of not trying hard enough to make the marriage work. Now you have the opportunity to show him that marriage is worth fighting for. Paul and Bettina didn't get married out of obligation or for practical reasons. In fact, they got married *despite* the impracticality of their age difference and the prejudice shown towards their match. That has to be respected as evidence that they love one another.'

Hammond sighed. He digested Jenny's words and accepted her reasoning, but there was a wave of nausea rising within him at the thought of growing old with Bettina as a constant presence.

'And what about children? Bettina is well past the age of child-bearing! She's old enough to be a grandmother!'

'But I'm not. I will make a great mum, Wally. I promise you. If Paul reconsiders my proposition, I swear that I will always allow him to be involved with his child's life as much as he wants. I love him, too. I would never hurt him.'

'Okay...'Hammond drew out his next question with hesitation. 'But isn't it a little incestuous to have a child with someone who you have always regarded as a brother figure?'

'No more than a mother or sister can act as surrogates. Instead of carrying a child on my behalf, Paul will enable the conception clinically. And anyway, it is not as if we are biologically related.'

She looked up at Hammond with such a yearning expression that he couldn't help but smile and pull her close in an embrace.

'I can't wait to be a grandad,' he said.

CHAPTER SEVENTEEN

His head was straining from the vomiting, but he was blind to the stench now. Elijah had lost all concept of time; there had been no changes in temperature or light since his abductor had left him. He had slept, woken up with the need to vomit, then drifted into nightmares where he was chased by demonic wolves. His body ached, his jaw was swollen, he felt the tip of a broken tooth catch his tongue.

He had fumbled his way in the darkness trying to orientate the chamber, but his memory played tricks on him. He tried to find the table and had searched for what had felt like hours until he finally grasped what appeared to a bottle. He ran his fingers up and down every surface he could find, but it took time. Eventually, he had managed to find three bottles and had lined them up by his feet.

He had been an idiot for drinking whenever he had felt dehydrated, because he had been under the illusion that the man would return, but he hadn't. Now he was thirsty again and the water had gone. He thought of the kettle and had eventually found it, but it was empty. He listened for any sound, but he only heard the noise of his own breathing and that became intolerable. Then he had shouted: shouted for help, then shouted at himself, shouted at the situation he had been forced to endure and still didn't know why.

Elijah had had time to think about the emails he had been sent. He had suspected that they had been harmless acts of ill humour by his old neighbour. The man had been an odd character, and been known to be quite spiteful. Mischa had shared conversations she'd had with his wife, in which Ellie had confided that her husband took pleasure in causing mischief.

Eric Winters relieved his boredom by spreading malicious gossip, but it hadn't bothered Elijah too much; he had excused the behaviour as advancing dementia. Susan hadn't been so sure, and had decided to use money as a ruse.

Elijah tried to rationalise the motive for his imprisonment, but he couldn't fathom why he was trapped like a helpless animal awaiting his fate.

It was too late now, of course. Elijah wasn't here because of a prank. He wasn't here to be scared. Eventually his concept of delusion and reality would become one universal delirium. He was now under no illusion that he was in this subterranean chamber for one reason; someone wanted him to die a slow and tortuous death.

*

When he heard the sound, he thought it was a hallucination, but he heard it repeated; it sounded like he was being called. The voice seemed to bounce off the walls, one minute seemingly far away, then much louder. He attempted to claw at the floor to pull himself to where the sound was coming from, but he was disorientated and there was no direction that he knew where to turn. Then he heard what he thought was a scream, followed by a thud.

Something vibrated near his head. He reached his hands out against the floor, trying to determine what had caused the reverberation, when he was shocked by a sudden whoosh of air that swept over him. He tried to open his eyes but was blinded by a beam of light that bobbed around him. Something was being dragged against him, something heavy. He heard a grunt, felt something sticky near his hands, and then felt arms underneath him pulling him up. The movement caused him to become dizzy and he blacked out.

CHAPTER EIGHTEEN

Hammond awoke at seven with a craving for cinnamon bagels. He had no idea why, but decided that stopping for breakfast at Costa before work would make a nice change. After all, he was about to retire, he may as well settle into new habits. He showered quickly and dressed in a blue shirt. Brighter colours were meant to influence mood, and he had read somewhere that the colour blue was considered to be beneficial to the mind and body by slowing the metabolism and producing a calm effect.

It was true he felt more optimistic; his conversation with Jenny the previous evening had helped. He felt guilty that he had judged her so harshly, although he did feel she was partly responsible for Paul returning to his marriage. Paul's change of mind had created utter dismay in Hammond, but he had hidden his reaction as best he could by shaking his son's hand and praising his humility. Whilst he would have preferred to have slapped his son's face with a wet flannel to bring Paul to his senses, he knew that Jenny was right. Paul had to follow his heart even if his father disagreed.

Hammond grabbed his car keys and called a greeting to the sofa as he headed to the door before remembering that Paul wasn't sleeping there any more. The sofa didn't reply.

Costa did not have any cinnamon bagels, so Hammond compromised by ordering a takeaway cinnamon latte instead, but it was too sweet and didn't have the energising effect he had hoped for. He reminded himself to buy some bagels when he went grocery shopping, then headed to the office. It was a few minutes past 8am, but the office was full. The room was buzzing with activity. Edwards was at his desk; he hadn't shaved and his greying hair was dishevelled. He raised his chin in greeting as Hammond approached.

'Did you sleep here all night?' Hammond asked.

'No, in the car.' Edwards raised a hand before Hammond enquired further. 'It's ok, I'll explain later.' He quickly changed the subject. 'There's a report coming in that the search team have found an unconscious male answering Elijah's description. Morris wants me to head over to the hospital.'

Hammond practically frothed in excitement. He headed towards the door but Edwards stopped him. 'Morris asked me to tell you to head to the old airfield. He is waiting for you there.'

*

It took Hammond less than twenty minutes to get to the old airfield at Lympne. He asked the younger officer driving him to blue light all the way. Despite the usual traffic delays, the journey was aided by extra compliant drivers on the road. The sunshine was helping to lighten the mood of the mass, it seemed.

As the officer parked the car in a lay-by at the side of the main road, Hammond got out and looked around him, soaking in the activity. There was a hubbub of noise, car doors slamming, SOCO officers unloading boxes and bags from their vans, radio communications stuttering, dogs barking or whining as their owners gawped on the pavements. Forensic vehicles and police cars were parked in the pub car park opposite.

Beside where Hammond stood was a narrow footpath leading into what appeared to be a meadow. Dog walkers were being turned away, but they congregated at the entrance trying to see the source of the activity. A black Labrador jumped up at Hammond, licking his chin in an over-familiar act of welcome. He gently pushed the dog away, disdainfully noting that the dog's owner was more engrossed in staring at the officers cordoning the area with police tape.

Hammond was directed three hundred metres further towards the middle of the field where Morris was standing underneath a Hornbeam tree. By his Superintendent's feet there was an opening that led down into the earth.

Morris looked up at Hammond. 'It's not him,' he said.

'Stadden?'

'Nor him. Chances are it is a security guard from the industrial estate on the other side. We don't know how he got to be here, though. There's no reason that we can think of, but at least we found him, whoever he is.'

Hammond peered down. Lights had been positioned at the bottom of an iron ladder that led into a chamber.

'Have you been down there?'

'No, SOCO will be processing it when they get here, but I've been told that there is a chamber about 110 square feet, with another hatch door at one end that leads to the tunnel behind it. The search operative had opened this hatch and found our John Doe lying there when he reached the chamber.'

'I heard he matched our misper's description.' Hammond deliberately avoided using names; you never knew when there were reporters around.

Morris gave him a withering look. 'No, this guy is dark-skinned, and he is younger than our missing man. I'm still waiting to hear whether he fell down the ladder and was dragged further into the chamber or whether he had been beaten. There was so much gore around his face and head, it was hard to tell.'

'Why wasn't I alerted sooner?' Hammond kept his voice light, but he was rather peeved to have been one of the last to have arrived at the scene. He was meant to be the Senior Investigator, after all.

Morris shrugged. 'Nothing personal, I assure you. I figured you would get here as soon as you could when you heard. You haven't missed anything. They can't tell us anything that we can act on yet. I just wanted you to be aware.'

Hammond thanked him. 'I really thought it was our man. Dammit!' He uttered the words quietly, but Morris heard and agreed he had thought the same. The two men stood to the side as the forensic officers started processing the area.

'So, where the heck is he? I take it the entire tunnel has been checked now?'

Morris nodded. 'As much as they could. Luckily, there were areas with enough light and ventilation down there, so it was possible to search more thoroughly than we expected to do.'

Hammond sighed. 'So, what now? Where else do we look?'

Morris rubbed his face with his hands. Hammond watched him and admired how the man had retained his good looks despite his advancing age. There had been a time when Morris had been a marathon runner, married, and exuded physical virility. But Morris had aged quickly. He had been divorced several years and didn't run as much, but he still looked good for it. The man had mellowed in many ways.

He and Hammond used to clash over their difference in attitude; Morris used to affect a superior attitude, whilst Hammond had enjoyed rebelling and acting on impulse. Over the years, though, the arrogance had dwindled to humility and the two men had grown in their respect for one another.

'I've stopped the search for now, since such a large area has been covered. I'll be distracted with another investigation for the next few hours – there's been another violent rape that I need to oversee. It seems it is the same perpetrator as a similar attack a few days ago. However, I want to have a detailed meeting about this later; every stone uncovered. Hopefully, Edwards will have more information when he returns from the hospital.' He turned to Hammond. 'Before I forget, Susan Maxwell's father is coming down to Kent tomorrow and I've arranged to meet him at 10am. If you are available, I'd like you to meet him.'

He was distracted momentarily by the crowd of people peering over the hedge along the perimeter of the field.

'There's going to be media interest soon,' he went on eventually. 'It won't take long before they start hypothesising that the man we found is Elijah, so his partner needs to be warned. I don't want her getting her hopes up.'

*

Hammond's mind was preoccupied as he was driven back to the station. He found he was noticing older men walking dogs and wondered if they were retired. Were they enjoying a calmer daily routine, or were they bored? He watched a father pushing a young child in a pushchair and imagined what Paul's child would be like. The thoughts mingled like the kaleidoscope of images that floated in the mind before sleep. He couldn't focus on one thought at a time. *Is this how it will be now?* he wondered. *Will my aging mind constantly flick from one thought to the next, unable to settle or focus?*

He arrived at the station and left a message for DS Edwards, then sought DS Williams who had been compiling a report ready for the forthcoming meeting. The younger man smiled and offered him a mint humbug, which Hammond accepted.

'I've concentrated all our findings in one summary. We have the information on the murdered pizza delivery boy, the past reports on the two other missing people, and Edwards has confirmed the identity of the man found at the airfield as a night security watchman from the nearby industrial site. He can't speak yet, although he was regaining consciousness when Edwards updated me. I think he is going to attempt an interview once he has checked with the medical staff.' DS Williams paused. 'So far we haven't found much on the Ghost Orchid group. I've located a possible address of a confirmed member, but they're secretive so it's not easy. However, I've been trawling through their social media pages and gathered information on those who have liked or commented on the posts. I should have more this afternoon.'

Hammond thanked him and headed back outside to his car. He stopped at the petrol station and headed into the shop, randomly selecting a packet of Rich Tea biscuits, and paid for them using the coins in his wallet. The cashier was irritated when he paid for the diesel as a separate transaction and gave an exaggerated sigh when she was asked for two receipts.

Hammond drove towards Mersham; he was nervous at the idea of interviewing Mischa again. He did not want to give the impression that he was suspicious, even though he had a growing sense of unease about her. He sympathised that the woman was in distress, but he was pretty sure she wasn't being as honest she could be. She had not responded well to being summoned to the station nor by being visited by the liaison officer.

He parked the car closer to her house this time and disturbed a squirrel that had been attempting to retrieve nuts from the bird feeder hanging from the bough of a tree. He watched it scamper up the neighbouring fir tree then headed to Mischa's front door.

Charlie barked a welcome and excitedly grabbed the Rich Tea biscuit that Hammond offered. Mischa looked surprised by Hammond's visit and led him into the kitchen but didn't offer him a drink. 'I'm working at home today, so it's lucky you caught me.'

'I'll be quick,' he said. 'I just wanted to tell you personally that we found a man at the old airfield in Lympne, as you may hear about it in the news. It's not Elijah and it may not be connected. We are not giving a statement to the media yet until we can establish facts, but it's possible that the reports will connect the two incidents.'

Mischa looked concerned. 'Who was it?'

Hammond shared the information he had.

Charlie had finished his biscuit and was hovering for crumbs. 'How is Charlie now?' he asked. Mischa shrugged. 'Still missing Elijah.'

They walked back along the hallway towards the front door. Hammond paused as they passed the living room, his glance resting on the display cabinet he had admired previously. 'Theodolites are surveying instruments, aren't they?'

Mischa's lips tightened. 'My ex-husband works in construction engineering.'

Charlie wagged his tail and accepted a back rub as Hammond bade them goodbye.

The squirrel had resumed its position on the bird feeder. He threw a broken biscuit on the lawn and smiled as the creature grabbed it and disappeared up the tree before Hammond had reached the end of the short driveway.

*

The team dissected every detail of their case notes. The thorough review took almost three hours, but as time passed the mood of despondency gradually lifted. Hammond's offering of biscuits had been welcomed as they sat munching through their deliberations.

'So, we've agreed that the motive is likely to be the intervention of the passengers on the Turkish Airways flight in November. The *Daily Mail Online* published an article in December 2017 that included a video of the protest. It had been uploaded by a passenger travelling on the same flight and clearly shows a woman and a man arguing with the Home Office Personnel. At one point, they are placing themselves between Petar Hovat and his guard, and behaving as a physical barricade. It is very clear that the protest is over Petar being forcibly taken on the plane. The article has quotes from Patricia Jenkins, who actually boasts about the role she played in preventing Hovat's deportation. She is quoted as saying she was, quote, *Doing her civic duty in protecting the vulnerable,* unquote. David O'Neal is also mentioned as having acted against what he believed had been an act of racism shown by the British authorities.

'The article mentions that Hovat had appealed to the passengers to help him, but it doesn't elaborate on his claim that he had been forcibly removed from his children. There is no mention of Elijah, but in the comments written by readers of the article, there is a posting from someone using the name Eric from Hythe that says, quote, *My next door neighbour was also involved. He was one of the passengers on that flight and is the type of man that would try to influence his ideals onto others. I would not be surprised if he told the others to protest.* Unquote.'

DS Williams stopped reading and offered a copy of the article that he had printed and enlarged. It was evident that this article could easily have attracted the wrong kind of attention. It certainly corroborated a motive, and had confirmed the link between all three missing people.

Morris was impressed. He offered Williams a congratulatory slap on his back.

Hammond agreed with the good work. 'I met Elijah's next-door neighbour. She did mention that her husband Eric disliked Elijah, so I agree it is likely he wrote that comment.'

Williams proceeded to pass on the notes about the murdered pizza delivery boy, now identified as Ethan Spencer.

'Because he was only seventeen, he was employed on a casual basis, which makes it even more tragic. His mother was at the hospital undergoing chemotherapy at the time he disappeared, so there was no alert when he did not return to the pizzeria. They weren't too bothered until they thought he had run off with the payment for the pizza.'

'Where did they find him?'

'About four miles from where he had delivered the food to Petar Hovat's address in Colchester town centre.' Williams consulted his notes. 'They found him near Langham Moor, in a disused building on private agricultural land, hence the delay. It would have been near impossible to locate him if Hovat's mobile signal had not been triangulated nearby. It took several hours to find him, but by then it was too late. The post mortem concluded that he had choked on his own vomit, but he had been physically abused and forcibly drugged beforehand.'

'What about his family? Any names that we can trace?'

'There is no father mentioned on his birth certificate. He lived with his mother, but she died of bowel cancer about three months later.'

'Have you found any names that correlate the missing people with Elijah?'

'I went with the idea that they may have been befriended by someone who gained their trust before abducting them, but I haven't found anything to substantiate it. Elijah didn't post on any social media, and Patricia Jenkins and David O'Neal had Facebook accounts but no shared friends.'

They continued analysing the various incidents, turning in as many directions as possible. Hammond didn't speak much; he wanted to listen to the details and hypotheses as they were offered.

'What happened to the money that Susan offered the email writer?' Edwards asked. 'There were no large withdrawals from her bank account, so does that mean she had access to large quantities of cash beforehand, or was she coaxing the abductor out of hiding without intending to pay at all?'

'There is still nothing to suggest that Susan's death is related to the same series of crimes. The foreign DNA samples that Henderson took from her body don't match with Mischa's or Stadden's.'

Hammond stood up and collected items from around the room. Moving helped him to think. He leaned over the table and placed various items in different places on the table, unaware that his colleagues were watching him with confused expressions.

A blue biro represented Susan; it was placed next to a red marker that represented Mischa.

A larger board marker was placed above them – Elijah.

Underneath, he placed four paperclips. One represented Ethan Spencer; another Patricia Jenkins; David O'Neal; and the last paperclip was the injured security guard found at the old Airfield, now identified as

Nicholas Adeyemi, who was yet to recover fully before he could be questioned.

In between the two columns, Hammond placed a short ruler; this represented the vigilante group Ghost Orchid.

During difficult investigations when Hammond had been unable to identify connections, he found that viewing each factor as physical objects helped him to visualise a connecting pattern. In this case, as he looked at the random objects strategically placed on the table, it was evident that they were lacking a centre, a common element.

Despite the subtle glances being passed between his colleagues, Hammond concentrated on the objects, moving them around in different positions. Then he walked around the table, viewing the objects from different angles. Then he stopped. His face contorted as he concentrated. He looked at his colleagues.

'The vigilante group... Ghost Orchid. Why name themselves after an orchid rather than something that relates to justice or people?'

'Apparently it differs from the more popular orchid because it prefers to grow in the dark. It is rare because it spends most of its life underground,' Williams proffered.

'Hence it is secret... unseen...' Hammond leaned on the table. 'What if the common denominator is not one person, but a location?'

Morris frowned. 'Each incident is from different areas. Ethan Spencer was abducted and found in Essex; Patricia Jenkins was from Surrey; David O'Neal lived in Croydon. The distances between each of them are too varied to form a connection.

Hammond held up his hands. The speed of his thoughts was gaining pace. There was a link; he could sense it, but couldn't visualise what it was exactly he was trying to see in his mind. He grasped his head as if to hold the thoughts in one place as he examined them. Then he saw it.

'Disused airfields.'

He smiled, despite the looks of confusion from the men seated around him. Hammond started pacing.

'Underground. Ghost Orchids are plants that thrive in conditions found underground. Elijah was taken underground. The security guard was also found underground, at the old airfield at Lympne. Our belief is that the death of Ethan Spencer is the motive for the three missing people. You said he was found in an unused building near Langham Moor? There is an old RAF airfield near there. The agricultural land covers part of an old airfield, and there used to be an old control tower that was demolished. If Ethan was found there, there is already a similarity between Elijah's disappearance and Ethan's murder.'

Morris stood up. 'I'm sorry, I don't see it. I think you are clutching at straws.'

Hammond knew he wasn't. The adrenaline that was coursing through him was making him feel jittery. He could feel he was on the right path.

'Please. At least give me a chance. Patricia Jenkins disappeared in Caterham. The old airfield nearest there is RAF Kenley. What if the old bunkers are searched?'

Morris sighed. 'I can't justify it based on a whim.'

'It's not a whim. It's instinct. I know it's an odd link, but I'm going by instinct rather than logic. Three people who travelled on the same air flight disappeared near airfields. It's the only common link; otherwise, it is one heck of a coincidence, and we know that there is no such thing as coincidence in police detection.'

There was a silent stand-off as both men eyed the other.

After a while, Edwards spoke up. 'The distance between Caterham and Kenly is less than three miles.' He looked at Morris. 'Do we try it?'

Morris stood, thinking, his head down, his hands placed flat before him on the table. Then he looked up. 'What's the nearest old airfield near Croydon?'

Williams looked up from his phone. 'Beddington Aerodrome. It has been partially used for redevelopment but there are areas of open land nearby.'

Hammond spoke. 'I think we need to aim for airfields that have old bunkers or subterranean chambers of some sort.'

Morris reluctantly nodded. 'We can consider it. If you find any such buildings, then we may be able to arrange those areas to be searched. So, does that mean we are looking at the Vigilante Group as being responsible for all three mispers? There lacks a good enough reason.'

'Administering their own justice.'

'There's a problem with that theory,' Morris stated. 'Firstly, it means they are operating out of their own area, which is unusual. The ethics of gang life or vigilante groups is pretty identical to any kind of clan – you don't operate on foreign territory. Secondly, the motive is too personal. If we can link a member to Ethan, that would explain it, but otherwise how would they benefit by administering justice when the actual perpetrator has since been charged and imprisoned?'

Hammond shrugged. 'Patricia Jenkins, Elijah Johnson, and David O'Neal were complicit in a murder that would not have happened without their act of interference. They would not have been reprimanded strongly by the British legal system that is sensitive to their democratic rights. Someone believes they need to be held accountable, and has administered their own punishment by making them suffer the same death that Ethan had.'

CHAPTER NINETEEN

'So, we are looking at the greater possibility that we are searching for three hidden bodies rather than missing people.' Morris's expression was forlorn. Eventually, he nodded. 'Fine. I agree we can talk to Surrey Police and advise them to employ their volunteer search teams to search the two disused airfields. Providing we get permission from the land owners, they can use the excuse that it is a training exercise. That way, if they don't find anything, no-one is any the wiser and it won't embarrass anyone. It will also mean that there will not be any media interest.' He offered a quick nod and left the room.

Edwards puffed his cheeks and exhaled slowly. 'My head is spinning,' he said, looking at Hammond. 'It all seems a bit far-fetched, yet at the same time there is a warped sense of logic in your theory.' He glanced at the deliberate placement of the pens and paperclips on the table. 'Your methods are strange, though. How moving items of stationery helps you to think of airfields beats me.'

Hammond shrugged. 'But we still can't explain Susan's death or locate Elijah. I want to find members of Ghost Orchid.'

DS Williams stood up from the table. 'I know I usually prefer to do the desk work, but I really think you should have someone with you.'

'Fine, we'll all go. What's the first address you found?' The three men left the room, fuelled by Rich Tea biscuits and a renewed sense of purpose.

*

'We're looking for an eco-artist called Thinx. They rent an industrial unit along here, number twelve...' DS Williams directed from the back of the car.

Edwards parked along a grass verge adjacent to a field backing the industrial development, so they were inconspicuous. The industrial area was long neglected. It looked like only a few units were still in use; most were boarded up and in a state of disrepair.

'Most of the businesses that rented here have moved to the newer development near the motorway junction. When the new television studios are built near Newtown, business will be booming. It seems odd that these remaining tenants didn't take up the opportunity to move as well whilst the rent was reasonable.'

Edwards turned around in the driving seat and faced Williams whilst he read from his notes.

'Thinx is a regular poster on the Ghost Orchid social media, often quoting Ghandi or Malcolm X. They haven't declared themselves a member, though, so they may simply be a follower. Either way, from their comments it appears they are aware of members' identities, which is why I think they could be worth questioning.'

Edwards looked at Hammond. 'So, how do you want to play this?'

Hammond suggested that he and Edwards question the artist but remain in visual contact with DS Williams. He didn't expect there to be trouble, but he couldn't waste time being discreet either. It was a matter of urgency; they needed to know the whereabouts of Joshua Stadden, even if that meant acting in an authoritative manner.

The air was warm with spring sunshine, and the sound of tapping onto aluminium sheets reverberated around the warehouse. Hammond called out politely until a dark young woman appeared from behind a large metal construction that measured about eight feet tall, depicting a female warrior riding a dragon. She was dressed in bright yellow overalls, her dark long hair intricately arranged in cornrows. Her appearance was strikingly attractive, but as she got closer to Hammond, his breath almost caught in his throat. She had the most beautiful eyes he had ever seen; light green marbles that radiated golden flecks.

Quietly he identified himself and Edwards, and explained they were hoping to speak to Thinx. She continued to look at him for a minute as if trying to read him, then her gaze shifted to Edwards. 'I'm Thinx,' she said directly to him, ignoring Hammond altogether.

Edwards shot a glance at Hammond, who couldn't help but gawp at the woman in a state of wonder. Her eyes really were incredible. He squinted, trying to see if she wore contact lenses.

'We were just wondering if you could help us locate Joshua Stadden.' Edwards smiled trying his best to be charming.

Thinx shifted her weight onto one hip. 'Why?'

'We have reason to believe he may be in the company of someone we wish to locate.'

'Why?'

Edwards suppressed a sigh. 'His friends are concerned about him.'

Thinx licked her bottom lip and turned her head slightly, as if aware their conversation was being overheard.

'I know Josh, but last I heard he was fine. I don't know who he is with. It's none of my business what he does.'

Hammonds shifted his attention towards the back of the unit, where there was an office area cordoned by a temporary wall. He feigned interest in the metal sculpture and edged closer to it as if admiring the detail, but his eyes and ears were more interested in the persons remaining out of sight. He was aware of at least two people behind the wall; there was movement, and the occasional shadow moved under the partition.

'When was the last time you saw or heard from him?'

Thinx shrugged. 'I don't know, maybe last week.'

'Can I ask where?' Thinx moved back from Edwards, then she glanced at Hammond nervously and turned her head as two men appeared from behind her.

'You heard her, she doesn't know anything.' One of the men advanced towards Edwards, eyeing him with a defiant look. He resembled an angry bulldog, short legs moving under a square-looking bulk of muscle that looked like it was about to launch at any second.

Edwards stepped back but continued to smile.

'We are not here for any reason other than making enquiries. We are not accusing anyone of anything. We would simply like to locate your friend that we know you were messaging a few days ago via social media.'

The latter comment concluded their meeting. Thinx exited the building, heading towards where Williams was waiting in the car. Hammond turned to follow her, but he didn't move in time before a fist connected with his spine. He recoiled in reflex as another blow came down on the back of his neck.

Hammond almost fell. He was bent over as the blows continued to rain on him. He wasn't able to stand upright in time to fight back, but Edwards had reacted, grabbing a ball pein hammer and waving it from side to side, shouting incoherently.

Hammond managed to grasp his opponent's thigh and levered himself to standing position. He slammed the sides of his hands against the other man's ears in a chopping motion, causing the other man to reel back. There was too much commotion to understand what individual action they took, but afterwards, Edwards and Hammond's agreed they had defended themselves as well as they could… but it wasn't enough. Somehow, Edwards had ended up bleeding on the floor. One of the men grabbed Hammond's inner arms and pulled them back as the heavier fighter threw punches at his stomach.

'Anything else you want to know, old man?' He leered at Hammond, his breath smelling of a mixture of cola and fried fish.

'Does Thinx wear contact lenses?' Hammond gasped his question before they dropped him to the floor.

*

The stab wound wasn't deep, but it looked serious when Williams saw Edwards lying on the warehouse floor in a pool of blood. The divider compass had been dropped on the floor beside him, and instinctively DS Williams collected it in a plastic evidence tube before blue lighting it to the hospital.

Hammond and Edwards were admitted to Accident and Emergency feeling embarrassed. They had achieved nothing but drama, and no progress had been made. Williams was encouraged to return to the station and resume his search for Thinx, whilst officers were to interview the known Ghost Orchid members as a matter of urgency, threatening arrest if they tried to resist.

The nurse examined Hammond. 'I'm satisfied your injuries are only minor but your blood pressure is too low; you're 80-over-60, which is worrying. I'd like to monitor you for a few hours before you are discharged, and then you need to make an appointment to see your GP in the next day or so.' He encouraged Hammond to drink water and have a sandwich.

Hammond left his bay and found Edwards lying on a gurney, wincing as he attempted to sit up without disturbing the new sutures under the dressing above his hip.

'Looks like we'll be here for a bit.' Hammond offered him a tuna sandwich which Edwards accepted. He looked grey. He hadn't lost as much blood as they had feared, but it had been a close call.

'I'm getting too old for this.' Hammond spoke with his mouth full, drawing the curtains closed so they could converse without being watched by other patients.

'You're ok. You're only here another week or so. I've got another ten years before I can retire.'

'I thought you loved police work.'

'I do, but it comes at a price.'

'Oh no! Not you, too! Not another marriage sacrificed for the cause.' Hammond finished his sandwich and realised he was still hungry. He considered going back to the coffee shop by the hospital reception and buying another.

Edwards grimaced. Whether if it was discomfort from his wound or from Hammond's words, wasn't clear. 'It's not the police work that is an issue,' he said. 'It's my lack of sensitivity and tact as a father, apparently.'

'Aha!' Hammond raised his hand as if saying he was guilty of the same crime. 'Join the club!' Then he stopped. He realised he was being flippant. Edwards was evidently trying to share something.

Despite his stomach encouraging him to get another sandwich, he pulled a chair closer to where Edwards reclined awkwardly.

'Tell me about it,' he said.

The time in the hospital passed quickly as both men used their recovery time to talk. It became apparent that Edwards had been struggling with his daughter's decision to change her identity.

Hammond remembered that his colleague had taken the day off work to celebrate his daughter's seventeenth birthday, which hadn't been that long ago, no more than four months. But as Edwards was talking, Hammond realised that he had not been the same man since he returned to work the day after Charlotte's birthday.

Edwards was studying a well-worn photograph that he carried in his wallet. The image was of his daughter smiling, her arms wrapped tightly around Edwards' neck as they had posed for the photograph.

'Charlotte was always happy to be my girl. She openly admitted she was a Daddy's girl; it was just the way she was. She used to love dressing up as a princess or a veterinary nurse. You remember her, Hammond? Charlotte was always a sweet, beautiful girl and was growing up to be a lovely young woman. A daughter I have always been proud of.'

Hammond nodded in agreement. 'Of course I remember. She's a lovely girl.'

'Only she's not a girl any more.'

Hammond frowned, confused. 'You mean she wants to be male?'

'No, I mean she doesn't want to be identified as female or male. We now have to call her Charlie, and I am meant to refer to her as *they* from now on.'

Hammond didn't know what to say. He could see the devastation on his colleague's face as he spoke. The tears were welling up in Edwards' eyes as he confessed his despair.

'How is your wife about it?' Hammond had always considered Edwards and his wife to be a good match. They rarely seemed to argue and whenever he had seen them, they were openly affectionate.

'That's just it. She knew before I did. Her gift to Charlotte was paying for her to legally obtain recognition as a non-binary identity, but she hadn't thought to share it with me. I had no idea that the name had been changed on the legal documents either.'

Hammond was quiet. He had been aware that there had been a recent flux of celebrities leading a new trend, mostly amongst the younger generation, choosing to be seen as gender neutral. Those working in public-serving roles had been trained to adopt gender blindness in the workplace and throughout their interactions with the public. It wasn't just a case of sharing toilets or adapting fashion to become less feminine or masculine; language had to be used with care and sensitivity. The changing of work ethics was problematic enough, but Hammond hadn't quite understood the implication before as a father. Now, though, it was evident in the desolate man before him.

'It was a habit of mine that I referred to my wife and daughter as my favourite girls. It was never an issue, just one of those endearing things you say to your family. I made the mistake of saying it when I got home from work yesterday. Well, you know what's like. I was tired, pre-occupied with the case, and I didn't think what I was saying. It just popped out automatically. Charlie yelled at me for being insensitive. The door was slammed in my face and then my wife felt the need to tell me that my lack of respect towards *them*...' Edwards made quotation marks with his fingers, '...was disgraceful. So, I was sent to sleep in the car.'

He shook his head and attempted to wipe the tears that were spilling.

'It is as if the daughter I loved so much has died, but I am not allowed to grieve or even remember her the way she used to be, because to do so is dishonouring *them*.' He uttered a sardonic laugh. 'I don't even know how to talk about *them* any more.'

He looked up with such helplessness that Hammond found he had a lump in his throat. He truly empathised with his colleague. Out of all the men he knew well, Edwards had always maintained the status of being the most dedicated and loyal family man. He didn't look at other women in an inappropriate manner, and photographs of his family were always carried in his wallet, in his car, and on his desk at work. Hammond now realised, though, he hadn't seen the desk photograph for the last few weeks.

He coughed the lump in his throat away. 'I feel for you. It sounds like a terrible loss,' he told Edwards. 'Your memories however are yours that you must retain. It's going to take a while, but you love her...*them*...' he corrected quickly. 'Charlie will be grateful and I'm sure *they* will recognise how difficult it is to accept such a change. It is going to take time.'

Edwards had begun to weep. A nurse stuck her head through the curtain and looked at Hammond almost accusingly when she asked if everything was alright between them. She left them, looking unconvinced by Hammond's reassurance.

Silence had descended between them. After a few minutes of awkward silence, Edwards coughed and blamed the recently administered painkillers for his emotional episode. Hammond agreed that they certainly didn't help.

He got up to buy another sandwich, hoping the tears he had in his eyes weren't noticed by the girl serving him behind the counter.

*

Hammond left the hospital at nine in the evening. Edwards was being kept in overnight but was expected to be discharged the following day. *It wouldn't hurt him to take some time off*, thought Hammond. The poor man needed healing in more ways than one.

The sky was still light with pink tints on the horizon; it would have been a pleasant evening if he were not feeling so bruised and battered.

Hammond walked slowly from the hospital to the 24-hr supermarket nearby. He purchased the usual groceries and added a packet of Nurofen painkillers, Arnica cream, and a five-pack of cinnamon bagels, before ordering a taxi home and claimed the journey on expenses.

CHAPTER TWENTY

Hammond's attire the following morning was not chosen with the same consideration as the previous day. As he stepped out of the shower on Friday morning, the bloodstained blue shirt in the linen basket showed him that it had not fulfilled its promise of maintaining a calm mind the day before. He blindly selected the first clean shirt in the wardrobe and winced as he buttoned it up, noting his stomach was bruised and swollen. Soon there would be less need to bother with buttons or even ironing. Once he was retired, he would get away with simply pulling a t-shirt over his head, and then have a whole day to do as he pleased.

He toasted the bagel and buttered it lightly as he looked out of the window onto the street below. A seagull circled outside and cawed loudly. Its secretions narrowly missed the window glass.

Hammond admired the clear sky and remembered his car was still at the station. He glanced at the clock and considered he had enough time to walk, if he left in the next few minutes. He quickly washed his plate and utensils, leaving them to drip on the draining board, and grabbed a light jacket, unplugged his mobile from its charger, and headed to the door. He paused by the sofa as he thought of Paul. The sofa seemed so much smaller and inadequate now. He missed his son being there. The door softly closed behind him.

*

Hammond was greeted at work by an email from the Scene of Crime Officers reporting on their findings from the subterranean chamber where the security guard had been found. The report was conclusive. There had been pools of vomit and diarrhoea found. Joshua Stadden's prints had been found on the furniture, the kettle, cups, and water bottles. Residue from the bottles matched with the analysis of the human secretions, and both concluded that Elijah had drunk litres of saline. The report concluded that the security guard had likely missed a footing on the ladder leading down into the chamber, indicated by the direction and amount of the blood splatter that had been identified as matching Nicholas Adeyemi's blood type.

There had been some blood found on the floor further into the chamber that matched Elijah Johnson's DNA samples, although it had been noted as a minimal amount, therefore there was no reason to suggest that his injuries were serious. Neither was there any suggestion that there had been any physical interaction between Nicholas Adeyemi or Elijah. The direction of drag marks in the dirt on the floor of the chamber had indicated that there had been a body dragged from the room back towards the ladder.

Hammond pondered over the report and forced himself to think positively. There was no conclusive evidence that it had been Elijah's body that had been moved, although it was unlikely Elijah would have dragged Stadden's body if he was weakened by severe dehydration. He could, however, be unconscious rather than dead, and possibly had been dragged elsewhere after being disturbed by the security guard. Again, there were too many maybes for Hammond's liking, but at the same time it was progress.

DS Williams looked relieved when he saw Hammond by himself at the computer. Hammond paused typing his report about the previous day's events and looked up to greet his younger colleague.

'I'm so sorry.' Williams wore a sheepish expression. He pulled a chair next to Hammond, sat down with his back to the rest of the office, and adopted a discreet tone. 'I tried to run after the girl, but I should have gone to where you and Edwards were. I left you without backup.'

'It's just as well you didn't see how badly we defended ourselves, otherwise we'd be straight back into the next self-defence training course.' Hammond smiled. 'Edwards will be sent home later today. He will recover quickly.'

Williams smiled, appreciating the lack of reprimand. 'I'm thinking of switching roles. I've realised that I prefer working behind a desk than doing fieldwork. Would you be willing to help me?'

Hammond studied his colleague. 'Of course, but you should know that I've valued your contribution to our investigation. I consider you an asset to the team.'

Williams looked surprised and went to continue the subject, but Hammond had already begun to focus on the work they needed to do.

'Did you manage to identify the two men who attacked us?'

Williams nodded. 'Yep. Thinx had recently used a loan shark, and those men were there to remind her to repay her debts. They have no association with Ghost Orchid. I have contacted Thinx, and she's coming in to be questioned later this morning. She thinks she is being accused of being complicit in the attack yesterday so wants to be seen to cooperate.'

'Excellent. Any updates on any Ghost Orchid members?'

'Yes, three were questioned yesterday evening; they all gave similar accounts. Joshua Stadden was in the pub with one of them on Sunday evening, but he did not mention his activities from days before to them. They said he was in a good mood, chatty and proactive with the cause.'

'What does that mean?'

'Apparently he gives talks on the difference between self-defence and vigilantism.'

Hammond raised his eyebrows. 'I'd be interested in hearing that. But he hasn't been tracked since?'

'Not yet. He has no fixed address. The people we spoke to said he is known to be a sofa surfer, but his description has been circulated so it may just be a waiting game.'

'Ok. I'm due to meet Susan Maxwell's father soon. I've had a thought...' Hammond remembered a consideration he'd whilst walking to the office. 'A theodolite is a surveyor's tool, is it not?'

Williams shrugged. 'Not sure I know what they are.'

'It's an instrument that measures distance and angles between designated visible points in the horizontal and vertical planes.'

'Ok.' Williams looked confused.

'I'm thinking... it is a random thought... but I saw such an instrument at Mischa Taylor's house. She has an antique collection of Victorian tools, and the theodolite was just one of them. It was a beautiful piece, which is why I noticed it. She said her ex-husband worked in construction engineering.'

'You want me to check him out?'

Hammond nodded. DS Williams peered at him with curiosity. 'Can I ask why?'

Hammond switched the computer onto sleep mode and stood up from the desk. 'Like I said, it's a random thought...' He left his sentence hanging when he noticed the time. He was running late. 'If you could just get some background details on him, it may make more sense later.'

*

Susan Maxwell's father was a jovial looking, portly man, in his early seventies. He introduced himself as Gregory and shook Hammond's hand firmly when they met him in reception. The men agreed on the pleasant weather outside as they wandered over to one of the visitors' suites where they were able to talk in private.

'The investigation into Susan's death is still ongoing,' Hammond assured him. 'We don't believe her death was intentional, but we are considering all possibilities.'

Gregory nodded, signalling his understanding.

'The Coroner did explain. They told me the circumstances and how Susan was found. In a way, I am reassured that someone allowed her some dignity at the end.' His voice broke. 'She was a good woman. I couldn't have asked for a better daughter.'

The man was grief-stricken but composed. He asked frequent questions about the police procedure leading up to his daughter's demise, and after the discovery of her body. He was concerned that Elijah wouldn't know of his ex-wife's death.

'I like Elijah, he is a gentle man. Not the kind of man that you would expect to get into trouble. I don't know his partner so well, We have only met a few times, but she seems nice enough and Susan spoke well of her. Has there been any indication that Susan's death and Elijah's disappearance are related?'

Hammond wanted to give the man more clarity but explained he was unable to do so at that time.

'I understand. You can't rush in and start throwing accusations or theories. My best friend was an insurance investigator. He often said that the investigative process is like doing a puzzle without a reference picture.'

Hammond smiled and agreed it could be a frustrating process. 'You met Mischa a few times?' he asked. 'She gave the impression that she didn't associate with Susan very much.'

'That's true. No, I met her through her husband. Stephen Taylor. In fact, I do believe I had a hand in her meeting Elijah! We met when I was selling my trout farm in Gloucestershire. Stephen was working on a proposed development site nearby.'

Hammond raised his eyebrows. 'Do you know what he was working on exactly?'

Gregory was surprised by Hammond's interest, but seemed happy to continue the chat.

'I don't know exactly. He was compiling data on the land nearby, researching the land features, dimensions, and so on.'

'He is a surveyor?'

'Something like that. To be fair, we only met when he was looking at the land surrounding my farm. The trout farming was becoming less profitable, and I'm an old man so couldn't carry on for long, plus Susan was not interested in taking over the business...' He realised he was diverting from the subject and refocused. 'Yes, I was saying how I met Stephen... Well, like I said, he was working on the surrounding areas and I mentioned I was selling and was considering moving closer to my daughter who was living in the South East. He said he was interested in moving to Kent and we got chatting, as you do.'

'When was this?'

Gregory pulled his lips in a pout as he considered. 'Must have been about just under two years ago, because I sold the farm in March last year, after a lot of hassle, and it took a long time for the paperwork to go through...'

'So, it was a short time soon after when you met his wife, or rather ex-wife, as Elijah's new partner?'

'Gosh, yes, I suppose it must have been! I didn't realise how quickly it had all happened, but like I say, I think I must have helped the relationship happen by introducing them.'

'Really? May I ask how?'

'Well, I had given Stephen Susan's address and told him to pop in if he ever was in the neighbourhood, and he did, bringing Mischa with him. They were separated so I wasn't complicit in encouraging anything extra-marital!' He smiled. 'Same for Susan; she and Elijah had been divorced for a while before that. I guess that is when Elijah and Mischa met.'

Hammond smiled. 'I guess so,' he said.

*

Hammond had not intended to rush the man out of the door, and worried afterwards that he might have given that impression despite his repeated words of appreciation for the man's visit. He had been pleased to hear that Susan's body had been released to her father for burial, and agreed to attend the funeral. Gregory Maxwell was a likable man, despite his tendency to waffle in conversation, but in this case, it had been to their advantage.

Hammond practically ran up the stairs and addressed the team with a renewed enthusiasm.

'Stephen Taylor works in surveying, so there is a chance that he had knowledge on the local landscape. At the very least, he may have been aware of the boundaries from the MOD land and the surrounding features.'

Williams agreed. 'I found the information that you asked for. Stephen Taylor works for Lowleys Surveyors, based in South London. During the last three years, he has worked on projects in West Sussex, East Sussex, Brighton areas, and Kent. I've compiled a brief summary of my findings.'

'Was there any mention of him compiling data in Gloucestershire in early 2018?'

Williams made a call whilst Hammond paced. His head was reeling again. The full picture was beginning to emerge.

Williams called, 'There was no work undertaken by Taylor outside the South East.'

Hammond beckoned him over to discuss the information that Gregory Maxwell had provided. 'Don't you think it is a bit odd that Mischa was introduced to Elijah so soon after he had met Maxwell?' he mused. 'It can't be a coincidence. What if Taylor had deliberately sought out Maxwell?'

'Why would he do that? Surely if he were after Elijah, he would go to Susan first or, better still, to Elijah directly?'

Hammond nodded. 'I agree, it doesn't make sense. If Taylor had encouraged Mischa to befriend Elijah, which is plausible considering what Maxwell told us, why is there the need to be so manipulative? It seems a long-winded way of getting to someone.'

Williams placed his hands on his hips whilst he thought. 'But what is the connection? How is Stephen Taylor connected to Ethan Spencer? Could he be the father, do you think? That would explain the personal connection.'

'We would need a DNA comparison to be sure, but there might be a quicker way. Look back at all public records that you can find on Taylor. Once we have a clearer picture, we'll bring him in.'

*

Thinx sat in the chair opposite him, looking as splendid as she had the previous day, only this time her demeanour was more amiable. She actually smiled as Hammond apologised for the way he had turned up unannounced the previous evening.

'I understand you are a follower of the group Ghost Orchid?'

'Yes. I believe in their cause.'

'Which is what exactly?' Hammond asked.

'Ghost Orchid tries to expose, or at least highlight, those who get away with breaking the law without punishment. Some people call them a vigilante group, but I personally see them more as a group who enforce recognition of the suffering caused to victims of crimes who have no closure.'

'So, what differentiates a follower from a member?'

Thinx leaned back in her chair. Her attitude was so unlike the hardened behaviour she had exhibited on their previous meeting that Hammond found himself wanting to know more about her. She was physically attractive, but he found her confidence and ease of being more appealing. It wasn't a sexual interest, more a curiosity. In some ways, she reminded him of Jenny.

'A follower can attend meetings, but they are not allowed to be involved in any of the exposé projects.'

'So, you are not aware of the methods that they use to expose the suspected wrongdoers?'

'I know they research the validity of claims via the internet, check social media pages, things like that. You should know that everyone leaves a trace of themselves without thinking. It's possible to see someone's habits or interests without them actually telling someone.'

Hammond smiled. 'Give me an example.'

Thinx returned the smile. 'Follow someone in a supermarket, for example. See what they look at, and what they buy. Two different things. They may look at an item and not buy it because it is too expensive or it includes ingredients that they can't tolerate, or they may be checking the use-by date and replace it on the shelf with the thought they can buy it at a later date. Already you have three possibilities: that they live alone, that they are short of money, or that they are planning to socialise at a later date.'

'Or they don't have a freezer,' added Hammond, and continued his questioning. 'But how would you apply it to exposing someone?'

'Easy. With repeated observation, a clearer picture of the person appears and you gauge their habits and their character: do they park their car in one space, or do they cross the boundary line without consideration for the driver next to them? Do they return their trolley to the trolley bay, or do they leave it in the car park? Do they take their own carrier bag or grab another, and if they do, do they pay for it or pretend they brought it with them? Behavioural analysis starts with observation.'

Hammond grinned. 'Yes, I can see the process, but it sounds a lengthy one. How long is someone under observation for?'

Thinx shrugged. 'For as long as it takes.'

Hammond found himself looking at her eyes again. He quickly moved his gaze away from hers and concentrated on the subject. 'Why are you not a member?'

'You can only be a member if you are invited to be one.'

'Are you likely to be invited? What credentials do you need to be invited?'

'Well, it helps to act with discretion, but also they tend to be attracted to people who have been victims of an unresolved crime or who have a particular reason to see justice done.'

Hammond considered this for a while. 'Have you a reason?' he asked quietly.

'My younger brother got beaten up on his way back from school once. He had his mobile phone and his bike stolen. He knew who had attacked him, but the youths responsible were only cautioned following a Police enquiry. I found the thieves and forcibly reclaimed my brother's bike. I did something that the Police were unable to do, because they could only act if my brother could prove the bike was his to begin with, or that he hadn't given it to them willingly. It was their word against his. I knew him to speak the truth so I acted in a way that the Police couldn't.'

'Even though some could argue that by using force, you were also committing a criminal act and were unpunished for it.'

Thinx's eyes glittered. 'Ghost Orchid know the difference. That's the point. The law as it stands is less concerned with the administration of justice, and more about what is seen to be politically balanced.'

'Ok, so when you have attended the meetings, are there people that you know to be members?'

'Yes.'

'Are these members local, or are there members from different counties?

She tilted her head to one side as she thought. 'I think a few come down from London for the meetings.'

'Are the meetings held in one place?'

'No. We get a text a few hours before, telling us a place and time. But they are usually about once a month.'

Hammond nodded. He was encouraged by the efficiency of the group. It was evident that there was a structure to how it operated and a sense of ethics that belied the group's cause as being credible.

'Joshua Stadden, do you know him?'

'Yes, he is one of the principal members. He describes himself as a politically intelligent justice activist, but from what I have heard he has low emotional intelligence, although apparently he cannot tolerate dishonesty. He was one of the founders, and now gives talks and organises some of the exposé projects.'

'Do you know how a project begins?'

Thinx shrugged. 'Someone nominates a person that they consider to be guilty of a crime. They have to have sufficient evidence to back up their claims. Joshua analyses it and decides whether it is worthy enough to administer alternative justice. If he does, selected members covertly observe the accused and report their findings to confirm the validity of the accusation before the punishment is administered.'

Hammond asked her to excuse him for a few minutes. He offered a drink to be taken to her whilst he hurried back to the office.

Williams looked up, his face flushed with excitement. 'I think I've found something!' he said. Hammond grinned and slapped his colleague on the shoulder gently. 'So have I. Do we have a photograph of Stephen Taylor?'

Williams printed a copy of Taylor's driving licence photo, and the two men returned to the interview room.

Hammond passed the printed photograph of Taylor to Thinx. 'Is this man a member of Ghost Orchid?' he asked.

Thinx studied the picture. She twisted her mouth and lifted her shoulders in uncertainty.

'I have seen him at meetings before. He was definitely talking to Joshua one time, but I don't know if he is a member.'

'One more thing: do you know how Group Orchid is funded?'

'Members pay a subscription. I think it is like £20 per month, but there are donations from private investors, although I wouldn't be privy to that kind of information. I got the impression that Joshua and a few of the other members take on special projects for private clients for a fee.'

Hammond wanted to kiss her with jubilation. He repeated his question about whether she could locate Stadden, but she insisted she didn't know, and Hammond believed her. Thinx looked surprised when he got up from the table and thanked her with sincerity in his tone. As he did so, he concentrated on looking in her eyes and left the room with the satisfaction of knowing Thinx's eyes were as God made them.

*

Williams hurried alongside Hammond, who was practically bouncing along. 'So, Stephen Taylor is a viable suspect. I found a very strong connection.' He hopped alongside Hammond, attempting to measure the older man's stride. 'On the public census for 2002, Stephen Taylor shared an address with Evelyn Spencer. He was living with Ethan Spencer's mum.'

CHAPTER TWENTY-ONE

It had been Hammond's intention to locate Stephen Taylor and bring him in for questioning as a viable suspect in the disappearance of Elijah Johnson. Hammond was now sure they were on the right track, and the feeling of relief was empowering. There were, however, still some unanswered questions, and Susan Maxwell's death was on his mind as something he needed to understand.

His thoughts had to be pushed to one side when he entered the office and walked into a bubble of intense activity. The meeting room was crowded with people, and Morris could be seen amongst the crowd, nodding his head as he was being congratulated. He looked up and saw Hammond through the glass door and waved at him to join them.

'You did it!' Morris slapped him on the back with such enthusiasm that Hammond was convinced he would be left with a handprint under his shirt.

'They found the body of Patricia Jenkins earlier this morning at RAF Kenley, like you suggested.' Morris motioned for Hammond to walk with him, and they retreated to his office where they could talk in private.

'Patricia Jenkins was found in an area that is beside one of the old dispersal bays. Nearby, there was a tunnelled bunker, which is usually sealed off, but it appears that it had been opened recently and then resealed with Patricia Jenkins inside. The search dogs picked up a scent rather quickly.'

Hammond screwed up his nose. 'She was deceased then.'

Morris nodded. 'Yes, has been for a while. There will be a post mortem, of course, but there were a few empty water bottles found with her and the initial inspection showed salt residue in them. Poor girl, it can't have been a nice way to go.' He paused and then smiled wanly. 'However, you have brought closure to her family. At least they can grieve; sometimes it is the not knowing that is harder to bear. I have to admit I am grateful to you for being so insistent, otherwise there is a chance she would not have been found.'

'What about David O'Neal. Still no news?'

Morris shook his head. 'Not yet, but I had the impression that they are allocating more police personnel to assist in the search now, having been encouraged by the find this morning. It will certainly help them to solve two disappearances in one day.'

Hammond sighed and sat in the chair by the desk without invitation. 'But we haven't found Elijah yet. I want to interview Mischa Taylor's ex-husband as a suspect complicit in the abduction of Elijah. It looks like he employed the private services of Joshua Stadden. There is no information of Taylor on the database, so I can't compare DNA with the traces found on Susan Maxwell, but I'm encouraged by the thought that he may be involved somehow. '

Morris nodded. 'Good. Edwards is insistent on returning to work this afternoon, so I've asked him to return to the hospital and interview the security guard. I've been informed he is awake; his condition is serious but stable. If you want to accompany Edwards, I'd be reassured we are not expecting too much of him. I'm not convinced he is as well as he'd like me to believe.'

Hammond met his superior officer's gaze. 'I'd be happy to assist.' He understood that Morris had also noticed a difference in Edwards' attitude.

Morris slapped his hands together and rubbed them as he considered the progress made.

'Great, things are certainly hotting up. If we can get Taylor and Stadden in for questioning, I'd be interested in sitting in, but there's not enough to justify an arrest yet. Our priority is still locating Elijah. It's been over a week now and I'm increasingly concerned we are looking for a body, judging by the forensic report submitted this morning and how it compares to the scene where Patricia Jenkins was found.' He murmured something under his breath. It had not been the result they had wanted.

*

Nicholas Adeyemi may have been a handsome man once, but Hammond doubted whether the man would look attractive again. His face was dressed in an assortment of bandages and dressings and he had recovered well from the surgery. The neurosurgeon had successfully repaired damaged blood vessels and had offered a positive diagnosis for recovery, adding that his patient had been lucky. But Hammond wasn't so sure that good fortune had been bestowed on the man; he had lost most of his teeth, but he was alive.

Adeyemi lowered his chin slightly to confirm his name and then used a finger to answer yes or no as directed. Edwards was a considerate interviewer. It was difficult to watch another human being suffer, but it was essential that questions were asked. The interview was a slow and painful process, but a clearer picture of the events leading up to the man's injuries was finally established. Adeyemi had been leaving his post, having completed his shift at the neighbouring industrial site, when he saw a light in the field that was the old airfield. Thinking it was lampers trespassing, he had ventured over to them but found an opening in the ground. Out of curiosity, he had crouched down to investigate and had become aware of someone behind him, but was unable to remember many details after that.

As Hammond and Edwards thanked him and replaced their chairs, the man thumped the bed for their attention. He indicated that he needed a pen, and carefully he managed to scribble a few words that made Hammond so excited he almost left the hospital running.

*

When Hammond phoned Morris, he was insistent. As many search personnel as possible were to be deployed as a matter of urgency. The incident vehicles were to meet them at the other end of the industrial estate by a row of old bunkers and hangars that ran alongside the main road. Less than a mile away from where the search for Elijah had been abandoned was an area where Hammond now believed they would find their missing man.

Hammond drove as quickly as he could, almost forgetting Edwards was still sore from his injury. Neither man spoke; the tension was palpable, as both considered the chances of them finding Elijah too late to help him. The journey took twenty-five minutes from the hospital, during which time the emergency vehicles had already arrived and officers were busy cordoning off the area as the search began. Police dogs whined and tugged at their leads as their handlers were set their individual areas, and set to work heading in various directions.

Hammond watched, alert to every sound and action performed by the search team. His attention kept shifting from the scene before him on the field to the control vehicle parked at the entrance where the search manager was receiving reports over the radio.

Later, Hammond would not be able to give a clear answer as to how long he had waited for the news. It felt like hours, but eventually he heard the radio stutter, 'Code Red.'

Elijah Johnson had been found.

CHAPTER TWENTY-TWO

Hammond's first sight of Elijah was as a corpse. He looked the colour of bluish grey, his forehead was distended above his brow, his lips and eyes had shrunken into his skull. Yet miraculously, he had a faint pulse. The ambulance left with Hammond and Edwards gawping at one another in a state of shock. They had expected to feel relief, but instead there was overwhelming dismay.

Both men had shared events in their careers that had left a mark. They had seen many dead bodies, horrific sights of inflicted injuries, the aftermath of numerous tragedies, but seeing Elijah for the first time was, for Hammond, a horrible experience. The only way he could describe what he saw was likening it to a scene from a zombie film. Elijah had reminded him of the living dead, only this scene had not been rendered through the artistic application of prosthetic make-up; it had been real, which made it worse. Knowing that it had been the result of an intentional infliction of a slow agonising torture was incredible. If the perpetrator had seen Elijah as he had been found, they must have a heart made from steel.

Hammond willed the image to leave his mind as he waited for the officer to create a common approach path, and then they entered the site where Elijah had been found.

They were taken through an old hangar that had evidently been used as a makeshift skater park. Graffiti decorated every spare inch of brick wall, and ramps had been made using various old materials that had been lying around – old doors, window frames, steel drums, tyres, and parts from an abandoned lorry that had been left nearby. Sheets of corrugated iron had been leant against an old iron gate that had been padlocked shut before the tactical officers had broken the lock.

He followed the steps that led down to a narrow, concrete walled room. There were no windows or ventilation, the only air that got through was from the stairwell, and the atmosphere was putrid and damp. Hammond gagged as he was taken to the area where Elijah had been found in his heavily soiled and unconscious state. The stain on the floor was fresh and still moist.

Hammond looked around, but there was nothing that could be of any interest to the naked eye. Any evidence would be traces detected only by the application of forensic science. His gratitude was signalled to the other officer with a nod as the room filled with scientific support personnel, and he left them to process Elijah's prison.

*

At half past four in the afternoon, Hammond received confirmation that the body of David O'Neal had been found amongst the debris of a disused hangar at the old part of Croydon Airport. Like Patricia Jenkins, he had been left to die from enforced dehydration.

Half an hour later, Hammond received the first report from the hospital. Elijah was in a critical condition, his brain was swollen, his kidneys were failing. His diagnosis of hypovolemic shock had been graded at level four. In other words, Elijah's chances of survival were minimal.

Hammond ended the call with a sense of renewed purpose. Where once he had been driven to locate Elijah, now all he wanted was to face the person responsible for causing such suffering. He was sensitive to the effects of grief and the need for justice, and he understood that the crimes against Patricia Jenkins, David O'Neal, and Elijah had been driven by a hatred for their actions. There had been desperation for them and others to recognise that they had been complicit in the horrific death of an innocent child.

Yet, Hammond could not imagine being able to commit such an atrocity himself. The image of Elijah developed in his mind again in such detail that he felt a wave of nausea overcome him. He made it to the toilet in time and retched loudly. The yellow bile in the toilet reminded him he had not eaten since that morning.

He sloshed water from the tap in his mouth and spat out the foul taste, staring at himself in the mirror above, and asked himself how he could contain his anger. The rage towards humans in general was rising within him. The constant reminders of how human beings treated one another was enough to make him want to hide and become a hermit, to deny his association with his own species.

But as he considered these irrational thoughts, Edwards entered the bathroom and fussed with his dressings that had been disturbed by his trouser belt. The action was so normal that, despite his despair, Hammond was almost bemused by how one life just continued with the need to complete menial tasks whilst another's could be destroyed by one thoughtless action.

His smirk was noticed by Edwards, who looked quizzically at him.

*

The team meeting was conducted with a renewed positivity; there was a resolution in sight. Hammond listed the topic that needed to be addressed. Now that Elijah had been found, they needed to continue as if it were an investigation into an attempted murder and a possible connected suspicious death. The team had already identified a plausible motive, they had discovered the means, and they had identified two suspects, now they needed collaborating evidence and witness reports.

Mischa Taylor was a witness to be formally interviewed as a priority. Hammond considered the time. It was reasonable to wait until the following morning before they questioned her, and he needed time to devise an interview strategy. It would be fair to allow her time to come to terms with Elijah's critical status before she was interrogated, but in the meantime they needed to wait for any forensic data. It wouldn't be available for a day at least.

Hammond thanked his colleagues with heartfelt sincerity. Each member of his team had worked tirelessly. He knew that often the investigations played on the minds of everyone involved, wondering what they could or should do to make a difference. Going home to their families at the end of each day helped to desensitise their work sometimes, but always there was the underlying preoccupation with other people's lives.

The team left the room with their individual tasks and a sense of relief that the investigation was beginning to make sense. For eight days their entire investigation had been based on theories, but now there was a clear objective. To get those responsible and find the evidence.

DS Williams approached Hammond after the meeting, and they discussed the written reports that were to be submitted. Afterwards, Williams hovered, scratching his thigh as if he didn't know what to do with himself.

'I'm not sure if I feel relief or distressed by today's events,' he admitted. 'We have helped to find three missing people, but each discovery was too late. Even if Elijah does survive, how will he get over being left there in the dark for days? It will traumatise him.'

'You can't think like that,' Hammond advised. 'It doesn't help the victims or their loved ones. Instead, you have to use your despair as energy that is better spent bringing a resolution.'

'If we find Taylor or Stadden, do you think a jury is going to convict them with a less biased mind once they know a child's death was the reason behind their crimes?'

Hammond shrugged. Such was the irony. Their suspects had wanted to bring about their own justice by hurting those they deemed responsible. But those they had hurt also had loved ones who would feel they needed justice if such crimes were not fully recognised. Where would it end?

Hammond imagined what his father would have said, and shared the wise words with Williams. 'Sleep on it, things may make more sense in the morning.'

Chapter Twenty-Three

Hammond awoke from the dream just as his mother was serving him clotted cream and strawberries, wearing the pinny he had bought her with his own pocket money for Mother's Day. He lay there, not wanting to open his eyes, and tried to hold the image of his mother in his mind for as long as he could, but she quickly fizzled out of his consciousness. She had been dead for years, but recently Hammond had found he was missing his parents more than ever.

The sadness came with the realisation that you were never too old to want the unconditional care and love that your parents gave you. Nothing could replicate it. Not even the love of a wife or child of your own. Hammond had been a father for thirty-three years and he had made many mistakes, but chances were that Paul would remember his fatherly advice as being the sharing of wisdom, just like Hammond thought how his father would advise him now.

In eight days, Hammond would be a retired man; in nine days' time, he would be sixty-one. The start of a new life was beckoning, but with it the anxiety that he would not know what to do with his time. Hammond hated the idea of wasted time or a wasted life. He needed to be fulfilled. For forty years, police work had been the one consistent factor in his life. His role as a parent and husband had dwindled over time. Lyn was no longer his wife, and Paul was married himself, but as a detective, his work had been all-consuming and had never lessened its demands. Without it, the days would be empty and uncertain, and the prospect was frightening.

He got up and padded into the kitchen, noting the washing machine had been flashing for attention since the previous evening. He turned the dial to the OFF position, pulled the clean laundry out of the drum, and decided he would move home as soon as he could. He wanted a garden to hang out the laundry and he liked the idea of growing his own vegetables again.

He toasted the last cinnamon bagel and looked out of the window. The sky was grey, there was a chance rain was due.

*

'I thought you might like to come to the hospital with me to see Elijah?'

Edwards smiled as he passed him, and Hammond found it almost unnerving. He was aware that Edwards was embarrassed by his confession about his family troubles, but he wished the man wouldn't be. Goodness knows, Hammond had brought his own personal issues into work over the years. He wanted to advise Edwards that there was no need to over-compensate by being so amiable, but decided against it for fear of embarrassing his colleague further.

He accepted Edwards' offer and enquired over his injury, which he was assured was healing well. The two men responsible for the attack had since been charged, and Edwards was looking forward to giving evidence in court. The attack against him and Hammond had been nothing more than a chance to throw their weight around, and bullies like that needed to be caged with their own kind. It was the only language they understood.

Hammond listened to Edwards' rant, and understood that the anger was a mixture of hurt pride and a need to masculate himself following his emotional behaviour two days previously.

Hammond took the road towards Ashford and Edwards' voice faded into a distant mumbling as he enjoyed the calming swishing of the wipers against the car windscreen.

*

Mischa Taylor looked aghast when she saw Hammond and Edwards beside Elijah's bed. At first, Hammond supposed the numerous machines and medical apparatus attending to Elijah were the cause of her displeasure, but when they smiled at her in greeting, she gave a nervous twitch of the mouth in reply. As she looked at Elijah, the tears gathered and she quickly wiped them away, aware that Hammond was watching her.

'Have you spoken to the doctor?' Mischa asked without looking at Hammond, her attention fixed on the prostrate unconscious figure in the bed between them.

'We've been told the consultant is doing the rounds but probably won't be checking in here for an hour or so.'

Micha nodded. 'Why are you here?' Her tone was blunt, almost hostile.

Edwards looked surprised by her attitude but remained quiet since Hammond had pretended not to notice.

'We're concerned naturally, and we wanted to be updated.'

Mischa raised her chin but didn't speak. She pulled a chair closer to the side of Elijah and laid her hand gently over his, being careful not to disturb the IV cannula. She gazed at Elijah for a long time and was silent, as if hoping Hammond would leave, but instead he waited. He sensed that it was only a matter of time before she would confess; she seemed genuinely upset by Elijah's condition.

Evidently, she did care, but she wasn't naive. Hammond had followed a trail and she had unwittingly laid a few breadcrumbs by her own mistakes.

A nurse came in and frowned when she saw three visitors, but Edwards flashed his card quickly and indicated that they were waiting for the medical team to update them. The nurse gave a displeased nod and fussed over the ventilator and IV before leaving them with a curt reminder not to touch anything.

Mischa eventually looked up and met Hammond's eyes. 'Will he recover, do you think?'

When Hammond opened his hands to indicate he couldn't answer her question, Mischa started to cry. She bent her head and wept over her crossed arms on the mattress, whispering apologies over and over to the unconscious Elijah.

Edwards decided he needed a coffee, so tactfully left the room, leaving Hammond alone with Mischa.

He walked over to her. 'He may pull through. He got this far, he's a fighter.'

'I don't know how I will ever be able to explain to him,' Mischa whispered. 'I didn't know he would take it this far. Truly, I had no idea.'

'That is what we suspected,' Hammond assured her. 'Mischa, can you tell us where we can find Stephen?'

Mischa looked up, her face a patchwork of creases and wet trails. 'I haven't been able to contact him, but when I last spoke to him he said he was going to a meeting tonight.'

Her face flushed like a child who had been caught with her hand in the biscuit tin. Mischa knew it was time to cooperate.

'Do you know where and when?'

She shook her head. 'No, he won't know himself until about three hours before.'

Hammond thanked her.

She studied his face, uncertain what he was going to do, but Hammond was expressionless. Unbeknownst to her, Hammond was questioning his next move as well; he wanted to know where to find Stephen Taylor as quickly as possible, but if he pressed her too hard, especially without supervision, he could be making more trouble. At the same time, Mischa was suggesting a willingness to comply. He couldn't arrest her until they had evidence she had been aware of her ex-husband's involvement.

He hesitated, weighing up the options in his mind.

'Do I need to come to the station today?' she asked.

Hammond nodded. 'Yes, we will be asking you to attend a voluntary police interview.'

Mischa offered a cynical smile. Hammond might have referred to her being questioned as voluntary, but even she could see she really had no choice.

*

As soon as Hammond parked the car, he wished he had stopped en-route for lunch. It wasn't quite midday, but he was hungry. Unlike his colleagues, Hammond had an aversion to packed lunches; prepared meals lacked the spontaneity of choice that came with the variety of local food outlets. The disadvantage of this meant that often Hammond was left hungry if he was unable to leave work, but on this occasion, he might just have enough time if he ran.

Edwards agreed that a warm pasty from the store over the road was appealing, and the two men considered their options before Hammond jogged over to the delicatessen. He bought a steak pasty for himself and then asked for a wholemeal vegetable for Edwards. On impulse, he added two jam doughnuts, and then sprinted back to the office.

The initial forensic data had been received and the team was discussing the findings. They all stopped talking as Hammond entered the room with a waft of fresh pasties and warm doughnuts. Tactfully, Hammond placed them in a drawer, pretending not to notice the sounds of someone's stomach rumbling.

'There were tracks leading to the hangar and along towards the padlocked gate. They appear to have been made from solid resistant tyres. There are drag marks from the gate down the stairs to the bunker where Elijah was found. This suggests that Elijah was carried from the underground room where he had been captive until he was disturbed by the security guard, and then driven in some kind of vehicle to the new site, where he was eventually found.'

'Or were the tyre tracks already there? By those using the hangar for skateboarding stunts?'

'It's unlikely. The traces left in the hangar were too numerous to process, but the shoe prints and tracks left by skateboards tend to be around the entrance and the middle section of the hangar, plus, they are not so fresh. Towards the far end of the hangar, though, the tyre tracks are very fresh and they run over some of the previous tracks. Secondly, these kind of solid tyres are designed for a high loading capacity; they are ideally suitable for forklift trucks or platform trucks.'

'Like an industrial vehicle?'

'Surely the industrial site has security camera footage we can access? Chances are Stadden helped himself and used a fork truck.' Hammond stated the obvious, his mind partly distracted with the image of his pasty becoming soggy from condensation in the drawer.

'Are there any other signs that it was Stadden who was with Elijah in the second bunker?'

'Partial prints on the padlock and gate. There is nothing to suggest anyone else was there, other than Elijah in the bunker.'

Hammond sighed. Secretly, he was disappointed. Providing there was clear security footage from the nearby industrial site, there would be enough evidence for them to justify a warrant to arrest Joshua Stadden, but so far they had nothing to implicate Stephen Taylor, other than theories.

'Okay, so what do we have on Stephen Taylor?' Hammond didn't expect an answer, but he needed to think, and talking was helping to clarify thoughts. He started to pace, one hand on his chin, the other seeking comfort in his trouser pocket.

'We know that Stephen Taylor was living with Evelyn Spencer in Essex for several years. He may or may not be the biological father of Ethan, but we'll presume for now he isn't, since his name is not on the birth certificate. But we do know that he was living there when Ethan was a baby, until 2009, so that's at least seven years he spent watching Ethan develop from an infant to a young child. That includes a lot of milestones in a child's life that Stephen shared; first words, first tooth, first day of school. There's an emotional connection. Evelyn Spencer died three months after Ethan, from bowel cancer, but had been receiving treatment for some time before that. Do we know when she was first diagnosed?'

There was a shuffling of notes before Williams spoke up. 'She was hospitalised for a colonoscopy in 2015. We haven't had much luck chasing medical records for her, but she had shared with friends that she was due to have one.'

'So that is a relatively quick decline,' Hammond sympathised. 'But that gives us nothing other than the idea that he was emotionally invested in the relationship whilst it lasted. He may have considered Ethan as a son, so it only gives us a credible motive. There's still nothing to link him to the deaths of Patricia Jenkins and David O'Neal. Did he have any work nearby, or can we trace his movements around the time of their disappearance?'

'All we have found so far is that he had taken days off around the time of their disappearances. There is nothing that we have found to link him with them, or for that matter Joshua Stadden. Surrey Police have sent us the preliminary forensic findings on the scenes where Jenkins and O'Neal were found, but most of the forensic material had deteriorated due to the damp conditions. The only viable trace would have been the water bottles, but there were no prints that could be lifted.'

Hammond was silent for several minutes. 'What I don't understand...' he shared his confusion with his colleagues, '...is the difference in attitude between the sudden disappearance of our first two victims and the long drawn-out abduction and torture of Elijah. It is more personal. Yet Jenkins and O'Neal actually openly admitted their involvement in the delayed deportation of Hovat. Elijah didn't. In fact, the only way you would know he was involved was through malicious gossip from his neighbour...' He left his sentence hanging.

Edwards spoke up. 'Jealousy, probably. That's the only option, surely? If it was Taylor, and that is still a big *if*, then perhaps he used Mischa to get to Elijah to get the truth, but she ended up falling for him. Hence, Taylor blames him for two losses, Ethan and Mischa.'

Hammond agreed there was a logic in Edward's theory. 'But they were divorced. He had already lost her in one sense.' He paused. 'They are divorced, aren't they? I mean, this was confirmed when Mischa's background check was done?'

Williams coughed. 'Not the divorce. We checked for any past criminal involvement, employment history, and bank records. To be fair, there was nothing that actually confirmed divorce status, although there was an entry on the HMRC notes that she had declared herself separated.'

'Not divorced? It needs to be confirmed either way.'

'And what about Stadden? Do we consider him to be involved in the other abductions as well?'

Hammond shook his head. 'Until there is sufficient evidence to link him to the other deaths, we can't assume he is involved. Surrey Police will be conducting their own investigation, so if necessary we can pass on any information to them. In the meantime, we focus on his involvement with Elijah's abduction and go from there.'

He was frustrated. All he needed was something that could confirm Stephen Taylor was involved, but so far there was only speculation and that wasn't enough to justify an arrest.

He looked at Edwards. 'The only way we are going to get the information we need is by asking Mischa Taylor.'

Whilst records were checked to confirm Mischa's marital status, and updates were sought from Surrey Police, Edwards and Hammond used the excuse that they needed to compare their notes. The second the door closed, the two men lunged towards the drawer that smelt particularly appetising.

*

Mischa had prepared herself for the interview. She was composed and her answers were carefully thought-out before she answered. Hammond had been seated opposite her for ten minutes, and so far she had confirmed nothing other than she had shared an intimate relationship with Elijah Johnson.

'How did you meet Elijah Johnson?'

'We were introduced through an acquaintance.'

'Who exactly?'

'Someone who knew my ex-husband.'

'Do you know their name?'

Mischa carefully considered her answer. She had seen Hammond lean forward slightly as if waiting for her to make a mistake and be caught out on a lie. 'I think it was Susan Maxwell's father.'

'You think, or you know? It was only eighteen months ago, not that long, or was the meeting with Elijah not so important, after all?'

'I know.'

'So, can you be specific with us how and when you met Elijah?'

'Surely that is not relevant?'

'It is relevant, which is why I am asking you,' Hammond answered calmly.

Mischa sighed as if the questioning was tedious and unnecessary. Her demeanour was so different to her earlier distress that he wondered whether she had been prepped by someone in the meantime. Stephen maybe.

'Susan Maxwell's father knew my ex-husband, and we visited Susan when Elijah was also there. We hit it off.'

Hammond smiled. 'You must have had instant attraction, but it couldn't have been easy considering your husband was there as well as Elijah's ex-wife. How on earth did you both know that a relationship between you was worth pursuing?'

'I don't understand what you are implying.'

Hammond leaned forward on the table. 'Ok, I'll be frank with you, Mischa. I find it a little odd that you were in the company of your husband when you met Elijah for the first time. Now, normally, yes, it is possible that you both took a fancy to each other, but to become a couple pretty much immediately afterwards suggests a very strong instant attraction. It couldn't have been easy for your husband to have accepted the situation, nor Susan for that matter. Surely there was jealousy or even suspicion from one party?'

'Not at all, we all got along.'

'But it was your husband who took you to an impromptu visit to Susan Maxwell's house?'

'It may have been.'

'It was or it wasn't?'

'It was.'

'But your husband had never met Susan Maxwell or Elijah up until that moment! It's odd that he invites himself to a stranger's house unannounced, with the specific reason of introducing his wife to them!'

'I think if someone had done that to me, I would have thought them rude,' Edwards commented casually.

Hammond agreed. He could feel the tension rising within Mischa. *Good*, he thought, *keep it going, she'll erupt soon and then the truth will emerge.*

'Well, it is just as well we didn't go to your house then!' Mischa retorted.

'But you would have had no reason to have gone to our house, because your husband wasn't using you to get information on us, was he? He was using you, in a way, pimping you to get to know Elijah and feed back any information to him.'

Mischa reddened. 'No-one pimped me! My husband was being friendly, that's all. He is just one of those men that enjoys meeting people.'

'So, is he still your husband then?' Edwards asked casually.

Mischa turned on him, confused. 'Yes, well, no, my ex-husband.'

'Are you sure about that?' asked Hammond. 'You seem confused. Are you separated or are you divorced?'

Mischa didn't reply, her eyes darting from Edwards back to Hammond. 'Why is it relevant?'

Hammond didn't want to play games any longer. He slapped his hand lightly on the table, but the sudden action startled her. The woman was fraught, her cool composure was slipping.

'Mischa, you need to understand that we are investigating the abduction and the attempted murder of your boyfriend. It is also worth reminding you that we began our investigation after you gave us reason to do so. So, instead of playing games, cooperate with us! If we ask you a question, it is because we believe your answer *is* relevant.' Hammond held her gaze.

'Since I have asked you to stop playing games,' he went on, 'I shall do the same.' He passed a photograph across the table towards her and leaned back further in his chair.

'We have reason to believe that your husband employed the services of this man, Joshua Stadden – a member of a known vigilante group called Ghost Orchid – to abduct Elijah. The reason behind the abduction is, we believe, an act of revenge.'

Hammond studied Mischa. She did not look surprised by what he was telling her. She listened to him, her eyes never leaving his face.

'In 2018, the son of your husband's former girl-friend, Evelyn Spencer, was abducted and killed by a man whose deportation had failed, due to protesting passengers on a Turkish Airways flight to Croatia in November 2017. We know that Elijah and two other passengers were somehow involved with the protest.'

Hammond gave Mischa the opportunity to interject but she remained quiet.

'My colleagues and I think that Stephen used you to find out information on Elijah. Perhaps he needed evidence that Elijah had been involved in the protest, because all he had to go on was a comment in the *Daily Mail* made by Elijah's next-door neighbour, who accused him of having initiated the protest. But unlike the other passengers involved, Elijah did not give any reason to suspect he had any part in it. So, Stephen, at that time being fair-minded, decided to use his wife to befriend Elijah and extract the information that would then decide if Elijah was guilty or otherwise.'

Hammond waited. Mischa had bowed her head and was now studying her hands. Eventually, she looked up and asked, 'If you know all this already, why are you asking me? Why don't you just charge me with being complicit in Elijah's abduction?'

'Because I don't think you knew how far Stephen would go to assert his revenge. I also think that, somehow, you developed genuine feelings for Elijah. Am I right?'

Mischa nodded, tears spilling from her eyes. Her breath came out in jagged gasps as she struggled to contain herself.

Hammond changed his manner, demonstrating his understanding for the circumstances she had found herself in. 'Mischa, too many people have been hurt already. Let them heal by helping us resolve this. Tell us what we need to know, please.'

After several minutes, Mischa agreed to tell them everything. Hammond and Edwards sat back and listened.

'Stephen and I are not divorced; we said that to make Elijah feel easier about getting to know me. He is respectful, so would never have allowed us to become close if he thought it was inappropriate.'

Mischa inhaled a deep breath then relaxed, as though she felt a sense of relief that she could finally come clean.

'Early last year, Stephen heard from his former girlfriend, Evelyn. She told him that her son had been murdered and she needed him to promise her that he would help bring justice to those who were responsible. She was dying and she begged Stephen to help, saying that she and Ethan could never rest whilst those who had contributed to his death were allowed to live their lives without knowing what they had done.

'Ethan was a lovely boy,' she went on, 'and Stephen adored him. He was the son that Stephen couldn't have. For a while, he was in shock, then Evelyn died and it was as if he became obsessed with the idea.'

She looked up at Hammond, eager to explain herself. 'Stephen had changed almost overnight. He was tormented, and the more he thought about it, the more upset and obsessive he became. I was scared he would make himself mentally ill, so I told him I would support him to fulfil his promise, but he had to swear that he would not hurt anyone who was not guilty. If he was in the slightest doubt, he was not to do anything.'

Hammond nodded, encouraging her to continue.

'He found an article about the failed deportation of the man who was later free to kill Ethan. It named the two people who were actually proud of what they had done. The fact that they were so boastful about their actions enraged him. He planned to abduct them and keep them in the same conditions that Ethan had suffered. I knew about what he was planning, but after a while he told me that he didn't want me to know more because that would make me involved. I had no reason to hurt them so it would be wrong for me to do anything against them, and I agreed.'

'But that changed,' prompted Hammond.

'Yes, he couldn't be sure whether Elijah was guilty. There was no proof, but at the same time, Stephen couldn't allow him to go unpunished if he had influenced the others to protest, like his next-door neighbour suggested he had.'

'So, you were asked to befriend Elijah and his neighbours to find out the truth.'

'Exactly. First, I befriended Elijah. But we were attracted to one another. As far as Elijah was concerned, Stephen and I were divorced, and I did have feelings for Elijah. Stephen said we could use it to our advantage. I was caught between two men that I loved. At first it was awkward, but after a while, it just felt normal.'

Mischa shrugged and uttered a laugh as if recognising the absurdity of her words.

'I befriended Ellie Winters, Elijah's next-door neighbour, and found out that her husband was renowned for being a manipulative gossip. He had simply written the article comment because he had known Elijah was on that flight. Elijah had mentioned it, but he had not known if Elijah had been involved in the protest. As it turned out, when I did eventually ask Elijah, he flatly denied any involvement. He disagreed with the actions by the other passengers and had been angry at them.'

Hammond studied Mischa as she spoke. He believed her. Her body language was relaxing the more she told. She was unburdening herself.

'So, what went wrong?'

'Me. I fell for Elijah, and I told Stephen I wanted a divorce for real. I couldn't live with the pretence any more.'

'But Stephen continued his campaign against Elijah?'

Mischa nodded. 'They say that the more you kill, the easier it becomes. I now know that to be true, because that is what happened to Stephen. He didn't have a conscience any more. He just wanted to hurt people that he felt were hurting him.'

'And that included you?'

'Yes. I did not know that he planned to hurt Elijah. Not until Elijah had gone missing. It was only when I saw those emails and I knew who had sent them that I panicked.'

'And you came to us?'

Mischa nodded. There was a pause; she was shaking. Hammond asked if she needed a drink of water, and they waited whilst she drank and composed herself.

'Ok, so you knew that Elijah was in danger from your husband. Why did you not simply give us this information and prevent it from going any further at the time?'

Mischa blinked. 'Self-preservation, maybe. I was involved. I was scared for myself as well as Elijah. I guess I kept thinking that Stephen would see sense, that once he spoke to Elijah he would realise that there was no reason to hate him.'

'And what about Susan? Did Stephen hurt Susan?'

Mischa nodded. 'Yes, but I don't know how. He told me it had been an accident, but he was angry that Susan had tried to buy him. She didn't know that Stephen was responsible at first, but he went there to confront her when he got the email offering money for Elijah's release. He told her about Ethan, but she was just fixated on paying money, thinking that offering money was the way to help.' Mischa laughed, shaking her head as she recounted the events.

'Stephen said he snapped when she offered to pay for a fancy tombstone, and then when he shouted at her insensitivity, she offered to fund a charity in Ethan's name. He lost it.'

'You mean he hurt Susan?'

'Yes.'

'And what about Ghost Orchid? Did you know Stephen had employed the services of a vigilante group?'

'Not at first. I knew he had heard a talk by someone, and it had left its mark. The speaker was this man here.' She tapped the photograph of Joshua Stadden. 'Stephen became more obsessive about the idea of justice. He felt the police had failed Evelyn and Ethan, and this man understood. I think Stephen just felt at last there was someone who understood him.'

'Is Stephen a member of Ghost Orchid?'

Mischa shook her head. 'I honestly don't know. The last time I spoke with Stephen, he phoned me and bragged about how Elijah was suffering. I managed to get him to talk by telling him I would come back to him if he agreed to let Elijah go, but he said he didn't have him. He referred to a friend, and said that his friend was looking after Elijah for him.'

'When was this?'

'Wednesday morning.'

'Did he say anything about whether he intended to meet this friend?'

Mischa nodded. 'He said that on Friday he would see his friend to give him the money that he had promised. His friend had earned every penny, and he wanted to continue to support his friend's cause from now on. He also said that by not knowing what had happened to Elijah, I would be punished enough, and as far as he was concerned our relationship was over.'

Hammond turned to Edwards. 'They're meeting today.'

Chapter Twenty-Four

'Do you believe her?' DS Williams listened to their account of Mischa's interview and questioned Hammond as he filled his cup from the water cooler. Hammond gulped quickly; he didn't realise how thirsty he had been until now. He pressed a hand against his chest as the sudden coldness travelled downward.

'Yes. I do. But I also believe that she is someone who puts her own interests first, so her account may be tending more blame towards her husband, although to begin with she was protective over him. She could have stopped this before it got too far, but as it is, we now have enough to arrest Stephen Taylor, and I'm hopeful that we can arrest Stadden at the same time.'

Edwards came up and handed over the notes on the Ghost Orchid members to Williams.

'Get hold of Thinx. If there is a meeting tonight, we need to know where and when. Thinx said that the information is sent via SMS a few hours before, so hopefully we can get her to share that. However, if we can get someone else that we know to be a member to do the same, then we can ensure we are not being given the wrong details.'

'Won't that cause suspicion amongst the members?'

'It could, but they only become members once they have demonstrated their loyalty. If there is an inkling that Thinx has given any information to us, they might feed her the wrong details to test her.'

Williams nodded and returned to his desk, where he immediately made a phone call. As Hammond and Edwards walked over to Morris's office, he shouted after them and gave them a thumbs-up.

*

It took three hours before they had the arrest warrants, but during that time the team had been proactive. They were ready to solve the case for good. Hammond went to the bathroom and looked in the mirror above the basin. He studied the old man who looked tired and in need of a glass of single malt. *Soon*, Hammond promised. *When this is all done and dusted, you will be rewarded*. The reflection smiled back in anticipation.

The text message forwarded by Thinx corresponded to the text sent by the anonymous member recently befriended by Williams. *'The Old Leisure Club. Upnor Reach. 7pm*

Hammond thought the other man blushed as he confided that this member would be a reliable source for any future observations on the vigilante group.

*

'...Man's greatest asset is the vehicle in which he travels his life's journey. It is the one thing that you can call your own. You make the choices how to use it, no-one else. To you, it is sacred; it is the home of your being; the one thing you can call your own. So, when another person decides it is ok to cause harm to it, or to control it as if it were at their disposal, you are violated. What do you do? You go to the Police, you ask them for help. They listen, but then you are violated again as your injured body is processed. To them, it is not your body; it is their evidence. When the evidence is provided at court, the jury of complete strangers look at these images of your body and they study it, and you are violated again.'

The speaker was a slim man with angular, gawkish features. His slight frame gave the impression that he was light and could easily be pushed over with the slightest breeze, but the passion that he presented in his speech was undeniable. He presented his speech with charisma, holding the attention of his audience by projecting his voice across the vast space which was packed with his followers. Bodies were pressed close together as people attempted to squeeze into the hall and watch this formidable character. The speaker scanned his audience as he projected his words, thumping one fist in the open palm of his other hand.

'...But the difference here is that we don't need the physical evidence. When a human being is hurt by another, the evidence can be seen in their eyes – an injured soul is obvious to those who can empathise, to those who have suffered also. If you tell us you have been wronged, we won't ask you to show us your scars. We will work together, not only to bring healing, but to give you strength that such unity of spirit brings, and then, we work together to find the wrongdoer and teach them the error of their ways...'

The clapping resounded around the hall. Hammond looked at Edwards and raised his eyebrows, the atmosphere was heightening. He and Edwards split up and shuffled their way towards opposing sides of the room. They had already identified Stephen Taylor, who was standing in the centre of the audience, hollowing his hands around his mouth as he whooped at the words delivered by Joshua Stadden speaking from the make-shift platform.

'Incarcerating someone for a crime in a comfortable prison cell doesn't work. It's too easy for them to sit back and play the system, pretending to change their ways, knowing that if they speak words of redemption, they will be free to do as they wish again. It doesn't work. Just look at the recidivism rates from the UK alone. About forty percent of ex-inmates reoffend within the first twelve months, seventy-five per cent of ex-inmates reoffend within nine years of release, and these rates are rising. Can a leopard change its spots?'

Stadden laid out his palms as he lifted his arms and questioned the audience, who jeered their reply in unison.

'No!'

'Too right, and a wrongdoer can't change their mentality. If they think it is ok to harm another being, the only way...' Stadden repeated the words with greater emphasis, 'The *only* way they will learn how it causes suffering, is to experience it the same way as they inflicted it on you. There is no reoffending. Once they have tasted the flavour of their own evil, they won't be able to spit it out; they will be forced to digest it!'

The clapping and whistling continued for several minutes whilst Stadden bathed in the admiration of his followers, then he raised his arms again and brought them down slowly. The audience became silent again.

'The law enforcement is good for us. It aids us and we are thankful for it. We are not to behave as if we are above the law; we aren't. British Law is for our protection, but only up to a point and it is conditional. You are paying for your offender to wallow in the comfort of their prison cells, you are paying for them to be comfortable, to be fed and educated. You have already paid with your suffering, but then you are expected to share your hard-earned wages with them as well. The average cost to the taxpayer of reoffending was estimated to be £10-13billion per year, and this is increasing.

'But we can stop this increase in its tracks by simply abiding by the law of conscience. If you have been wronged, share it with us. Those who did you wrong, tell us about them. We may not have all the answers, but we understand. We know what it is to suffer at the hands of others, and we know that when those who do wrong go unpunished, it causes greater harm; it eats at the souls of the wounded. We are not going to suffer any longer. We will defend ourselves and our right to strike at the heart of the beast called injustice.'

Stadden stepped back as he raised his arms again. He was smiling, enjoying the limelight, and the audience was hyped and excited.

Hammond tiptoed to see above the bouncing heads and shoulders that were pushing towards Stadden and managed to make eye contact with Williams, who then signalled to the undercover officers at the side of the platform. As Stadden stepped off into the embrace of the crowd, Hammond moved forwards so that he was right beside him. At that same moment, Edwards and another officer had reached the sides of Taylor.

The situation was tense. A public arrest amongst a crowd of vigilantes was risky, but the team had devised a method of doing so without causing too much notice. They couldn't arrest either man until they had witnessed a transaction between them. So, they remained as close as they dared.

Morris and other plain-clothed officers were on standby outside the hall, all the while remaining vigilant and supervising any means of exit. It was not possible to talk over a radio, the sound was too deafening, and it was essential they did not create a riot by charging in waving handcuffs. The only way was to be patient and wait for the excitement in the room to calm.

Stadden was being congratulated by hearty exclamations and slaps on the back when Taylor sidled up closer, Edwards not far behind. As the majority of the audience headed towards the main door, Hammond and his team had subtly herded Stadden and Taylor to the corner nearest the platform. This gave them the best advantage of witnessing any transaction between their two suspects, and also meant that they could act as a barrier should either man attempt to flee.

Within minutes, Stephen Taylor had shaken the hand of his idol, and Stadden whispered in his ear. Hammond presumed these must have been words of encouragement, as Taylor was grinning and shaking his head with excitement. The two men laughed and then Taylor did as he was expected. He reached into the pocket of his trousers and handed Stadden an envelope. The two men conversed, and Stadden bowed his head in a humbling expression, as if he had received a compliment.

Stadden opened the envelope. Hammond had stopped breathing; he needed to see the contents to be sure, but Stadden didn't pull anything out of the package.

Hammond eyed Edwards, urging him to wait. As they stood, almost frozen, people were shifting around them, their barrier was being dispersed, and Stadden was becoming distracted as he was being called over towards the main entrance. Hammond nodded at his colleagues; it was now or never.

They swooped in towards Taylor and Stadden in one sudden movement, clasping the men's arms behind their backs, and quickly reciting their rights as they marched them towards the nearest fire exit. Morris saw them and called for the van to be driven closer to the door.

Taylor started to shout but the sound of the crowd was too loud for his words to be decipherable until it was too late. By the time the crowd had turned and noticed the van, the doors were already being slammed closed. Joshua Stadden and Stephen Taylor had been successfully apprehended.

*

Stephen Taylor had once been a man with a conscience. He had been loved and respected by many, but multiple bereavements of what had once been two family members, plus the emotional loss of his wife, in a short amount of time, had contributed to a loss of balance. Exaggerated grief had most likely contributed to a psychiatric disorder, and as such, it was necessary for him to be assessed by a psychiatrist before he was to be considered fit enough for an interview.

Joshua Stadden, however, was more than willing to assist the police by answering their questions. He had sat in the interviewing room with his legs spread apart, his arms open and hands laid flat on the table. His confidence and his willingness to answer demonstrated his belief that he had acted in good conscience. He pointed out that he had simply been employed to guide Elijah through a series of tunnels, and to keep him safe until he was to be met by Stephen Taylor.

There was no evidence that Elijah had been taken against his will, nor was there any evidence that Stadden had contaminated the water bottles with salt. On the contrary, he had been most hospitable by making Elijah a cup of tea and offering him refreshments to make him more comfortable. If he had hurt Elijah by striking him, it was in self-defence, after Elijah had attempted to fight. Stadden denied any knowledge of the deaths of Patricia Jenkins and David O' Neal, and it was credible that he'd had no involvement in their deaths or their abductions. The four thousand pounds in cash given to Stadden by Stephen Taylor had been a donation to Ghost Orchid towards their cause.

The only time Joshua Stadden's composure slipped was when Morris referred to the footage posted on Stadden's social media, where he and his fellow members had intercepted a boat of migrants on the South coast-line and had deliberately overturned them, leaving them to drown. Stadden denied that this had been an act of racism, but explained that it was the responsibility of the UK Border Agency to police the borders around the UK. If migrants chose to ignore the laws that were in place for their protection as well as the natives, then they should be reminded that there were penalties for disrespecting the need to abide, he told them. Stadden added as an afterthought that rather than leave the people to drown, he had simply left them to receive aid from the coastguard.

The interview had lasted forty minutes, after which Hammond's mind was reeling with the arrogance of the man. What made it worse was that Joshua Stadden was probably right. Whilst there was enough evidence to charge him, his conviction would depend on how easily a jury could be convinced that his actions had been hostile towards Elijah. The CCTV footage from the industrial development was limited; it showed a hooded figure drive a forklift off the site, but it was enough to substantiate that a forklift had been used to transport Elijah from the Old Airfield tunnel entrance to the disused bunkers nearby.

As Hammond and the team discussed the case, they had to admit that while there were still issues that needed clarification, nothing more could be done until they could interview Stephen Taylor and get a statement from Elijah Johnson, who remained in critical condition.

Hammond left the team to conclude their reports and went to phone Gregory Maxwell. The man needed to know what had happened to his daughter, and Hammond explained as sensitively as he could the circumstances that had led to Susan's death, sharing the information that the foreign DNA found on Susan's body had matched Stephen's Taylor's sample. He ended the call promising to update the man once Stephen Taylor had been interviewed, but appreciated how Maxwell was sympathetic towards Taylor. Susan's father empathised rather than resented the man whose grief had become overwhelming.

*

When Hammond sent his report to Morris at ten o'clock that evening, he found his hands hovered over the computer keyboard for a prolonged duration. There was a desire to continue the report, but he had to accept that it could not be concluded with the result he had hoped for. He sat at his desk for a while, acknowledging his colleagues as they left for home. Eventually the office was empty.

Hammond stayed. The feeling in his chest was not relief, but it was the closest he would get to the feeling of acceptance that nothing more could be done. He and the team had succeeded in bringing closure; Elijah Johnson had been found, and those responsible for his disappearance would be held accountable for their actions, but there had been too many victims.

It never ceased to amaze Hammond how one action towards another human being could create a domino effect. The first assault by Petar Hovat had led to the subsequent deaths of Ethan Spencer, Patricia Jenkins, David O'Neal, Susan Maxwell, and additional harm to Stephen Taylor, Elijah Johnson, Mischa Taylor, and Nicholas Adeyemi. Hammond spoke their names aloud to the empty room; he wanted them to be acknowledged. All of them were victims.

Hammond sighed. His forty years of police work had to be concluded with the acceptance that he would never be able to answer the question asked by every victim: why?

CHAPTER TWENTY-FIVE

It was Hammond's last week as a police officer, and most of that week had been spent doing what Morris had referred to as 'tying up loose ends'. In other words, it meant the submission of reports and debriefing prosecutors as to who had done what, being clear about the hows and the whys. It was a tedious process, but it was necessary. The task of justifying every action helped to bring a sense of closure, which is what Hammond needed as much as anyone. He couldn't anticipate what his days would be like a week later, but he guessed that he wouldn't be able to tolerate the idea that he had left something unchecked.

On the afternoon of Thursday, 25th April, Hammond accepted a glass of scotch in the privacy of Morris's office. The two men clinked their glasses in mutual respect and were quiet for a while until Hammond found himself smiling with amusement.

Morris enquired why with a raised brow.

'I would never have predicted you and I sitting together in such harmony,' Hammond chuckled. He looked down at his glass, surprised by the speed at which he had emptied it.

Morris refilled the glass and sat back in his chair. 'I would call it more a case of having different methodologies.'

'You were a climber; I was happier with my feet on solid ground.'

Morris offered a wry smile. 'Like a pig in muck.'

'We can't all go around looking like a film star,' Hammond retorted.

There had been a time when Morris had intimidated Hammond with his physical prowess, but good looks hadn't made life any easier for the man. He had ended up more or less in the same position as Hammond. He was higher up the ranks and he had a better salary, but ultimately, he had turned into a single, lonely, work obsessive, and as such the two men viewed each other as equals.

They downed their drinks before Hammond stood up and returned the chair against the wall. 'Tomorrow I'm looking at houses, and then I'll go and buy myself a suit for the party. Heck, I may even buy some new socks for the occasion!'

Morris stood and grasped Hammond's hand with both of his own. They shook hands in such a way that Hammond left the office feeling as if he had just bade goodbye to a dear friend.

*

Despite Hammond's intention to sleep late, he arose from bed before seven in the morning, enjoyed a hot shower and shave, and decided he would enjoy a cooked breakfast in the bistro in the old part of the high street. It was just after nine when he walked into the first estate agents he came across. He announced that he wanted to sell his flat, but it was important he had a quick sell, even if that meant accepting a price below its true value. He arranged for the agent to do an appraisal that afternoon, then he sauntered over to the harbour and sat listening to the seagulls and the bustle of town activity.

He took the time to watch a couple walking on the beach with an excitable Jack Russell and wondered about Charlie, hoping that he and Elijah would be reunited. The thought of the little dog being left alone brought a lump to his throat. *I'm getting too emotional*, he thought. *It must be age.*

The couple took it in turns to throw a ball for the dog to chase. It was a repetitive game, yet the dog didn't get bored. Every time it returned the ball, it would sit in anticipation for it to be thrown again, its tail wagging so fast it looked like a propeller.

Occasionally the couple demonstrated affection with one another, kissing and holding hands, and as Hammond watched them he found himself wondering if he would be spending the rest of his life as a single man. He had not anticipated how his life would unfold, but now he was on the precipice of a new beginning, there was the feeling that anything was possible. The image of Alice emerged in his mind, and he found himself smiling at the thought of seeing her.

*

The man in the mirror looked handsome. The stone coloured linen suit was a slim fit, and was complimented by a blue and white striped shirt, and brown leather belt with matching shoes. His new socks were somewhat of a luxury, branded with a designer name that was unfamiliar, but they were beautifully soft. He had cut his toenails especially for the occasion.

Hammond studied himself and questioned whether he looked like a man about to turn sixty-one; he didn't think he looked old, but he had developed a cragginess to his features that he hadn't noticed before.

His mobile beeped. Paul had arrived at the hotel and was warning him that the room was packed with people all waiting to give him their best wishes. Hammond checked the time. His guests were early; the party was not due to start for another half an hour. He texted that he was on his way, wished his reflection good luck, and left the apartment.

*

Hammond was aware he was getting more emotional, but he had not expected to be overwhelmed with such a mixed feeling of sadness and appreciation for everyone in the room. He had almost welled up when he saw former Superintendent Philip Beech, who practically sprinted across the room and embraced Hammond, slapping him on the back with excessive enthusiasm.

'Welcome to the club!' Beech chortled loudly, and proceeded to guide Hammond around the room, telling everyone they came across all the antics that the younger Detective Hammond had got up to whilst under his command.

Lois Dunn looked sensational in a lime green dress with a plunging neckline. She was delighted to see Hammond again and just as excited to see Edwards, exclaiming how quickly his hair had greyed.

Hammond enjoyed the laughter and the banter of all his friends and colleagues, but after a while began to feel embarrassed by all the attention that was lavished on him. He made his excuses and ventured over to the bar, where a woman in her mid-thirties was seated, looking lost.

As Hammond approached, he stopped, questioning whether his eyes were deceiving him. 'Mrs Galvin?'

The woman met his gaze and immediately got off her stool, walking over to him with a smile and an outstretched hand, which he shook warmly and then pulled her in for a quick embrace. She returned the greeting with mutual affection.

'Please call me Anne,' she said shyly.

'Anne, it is wonderful to see you, truly it is. How's young Michael?'

'He's good. He's a proper young man now.'

Hammond nodded and looked thoughtful. 'Crikey, yes, he must be about ten now?' Anne Galvin nodded, and they laughed awkwardly. 'There isn't a day when I don't think of Michael,' Hammond admitted. 'He had such a zest for police work, he would probably have been a DCI by now.'

Anne laughed. She recognised the sadness in Hammond's eyes as he thought of his younger former colleague. DS Michael Galvin. He had been anticipating the birth of his first born when, just as he had heard the news he was a father, he had been killed by a man whom Hammond had stubbornly insisted on following without waiting for back-up. It was, and would always be, one of the biggest regrets of Hammond's life. Even though he had long been cleared of responsibility for Galvin's death, Hammond had never forgiven himself.

Anne squeezed Hammond's forearm. 'Thank you for the birthday cards and money you send to Michael Junior every year. Many people forgot after a few years;

they moved on, but you haven't. I know young Michael doesn't know you very well, but I wanted you to know how much we appreciate you keeping in touch, and how we both wish you a wonderful retirement. You deserve a rest now.' She paused. 'What will you do now?'

Hammond laughed. 'I have absolutely no idea!' Then he bent over towards her ear as if confiding a secret, and pointed discreetly towards where Paul was talking to Lois Dunn. 'I'm hoping to be a grandfather soon, so I'm guessing I will be occupied somehow!'

Anne smiled. 'Oh, in that case, I wish you a lot of luck as well as happiness.' They toasted each other's happiness and Hammond downed his whisky in one gulp.

*

Paul dragged Hammond into his living room just after midnight. After several failed attempts to lift his father onto the sofa, he eventually propped him against the furniture and surrounded his unconscious body with the soft cushions. Paul sat on the chair opposite, listening to his father snoring. He had enjoyed his evening; it had been the first time that he had seen his father in his role as a detective, and he had not realised how respected his dad was.

Throughout the evening he had been approached by many people who had recounted their experiences working alongside Detective Hammond. He had heard how many lives had been affected by his father's kindness and his persistence, how his father would work tirelessly to solve a case – sometimes to his own detriment, and had been told about his father's' numerous blunders, and humorous accounts of arguments he'd had with colleagues.

He had heard tragic tales of loss that his father had endured, such as the deaths of his former Detective Inspector Harris, and Detective Sergeant Galvin. There had been a side to his father that Paul had never seen until tonight. Until now, Hammond had always been Dad – a pre-occupied, bumbling, heavy-footed, emotionally sensitive, embarrassing dad. As he remembered details of the evening, Paul was overcome with emotion. He hadn't realised how proud he was of his father until that moment.

He got up from the armchair and kissed his father's forehead. 'Happy birthday, old man,' he whispered, then left Hammond to sleep off the effects of excess whisky.

On his sixty-first birthday, Wallace Hammond's new life had begun.

EPILOGUE

According to statistical averages, most British people move home eight times during the course of their lives. This made Hammond the exception; he had moved home only four times before now. This new home he was about to take residence in would be his fifth, and hopefully his last, move. He had selected the two-bedroom cottage near Deal with the intention of growing old there, possibly even dying in the glazed loggia that allowed a glimpse of the sea.

Hammond had no intention of moving again; this would be the last time. As he contemplated the boxes that he was packing with his few possessions, he found himself recognising the advantage of having lost most of his treasured collectables in the house fire nine years previously. It had been a heart-wrenching loss of photo albums, the usual decorative ornaments and trinkets given to him by Paul or Lyn over the years, and classical literature including some first editions. The destruction of his vinyl collection had caused the greatest regret, but at least now he didn't have to pack clutter. All he was taking to his new life were the basic essentials. In time, he might find replacements, but there was also the opportunity to start afresh.

Hammond felt jittery with excitement; he was looking forward to taking up residency in a place that already felt like home. When he had moved into the

Folkestone apartment, he had done so for practical reasons, but he had grown to hate it. During the eight years he had lived overlooking the harbour, he had not shared any happy memories with anyone within the cramped abode.

But this new cottage had already offered some hope of happiness. Alice had agreed to come and view the new house at his invitation. She wanted to wait until he had taken possession, but she was looking forward to Hammond entertaining her there. Just thinking of it made him smile. Alice was a lovely woman; she was gentle and sweet natured, and her shyness was rather endearing. He hoped that he would be allowed the opportunity to get to know her better.

So far, he had only shared a meal with her, and they had exchanged the usual introductory facts about themselves, but he looked forward to knowing her better. He suspected there was a highly astute and fun-loving character hidden under the nervous giggle and quick wit.

Hammond stood up and tentatively shuffled another box over to the wall, aware that his back was aching. The last thing he wanted was to strain a muscle just as he was about to load the hire van. He peered out the window looking to see if Paul had parked the vehicle nearby. It was always difficult to park along the harbour road, and he dreaded the thought of the two of them having to carry furniture along the main road.

Hammond returned to the kitchen and scanned the room, ensuring he had not left any trace of himself behind. He left a bottle of champagne for the new owner in the fridge, and balanced a greeting card next to it. Then he examined the bathroom, double checking the toilet and all the plug holes were free of hair or debris. He used the cuff of his jumper to wipe a smidgeon of a print visible on the chrome tap, and congratulated himself for having left the rooms looking spotless.

Hammond's mobile rang, and within a few minutes he was smiling. His money had been received by the seller and the keys were ready to be handed over. He rubbed his hands together and danced a little jig just as Paul walked in the door

*

The new headlines were focused on the Brexit blame game, so Hammond turned the pages quickly and settled on an article that reported Tardigrades had likely taken up residency on the moon following their crash landing on an Israeli spacecraft four months earlier. Whilst it was a breakthrough in science, it meant that the Outer Space Treaty had been breached due to contaminating the otherwise pristine environment of the moon.

Hammond sipped his coffee and debated aloud to an empty room that, in his opinion, Neil Armstrong and Buzz Aldrin had already done that when they raised the American flag at their landing site.

From his position seated at the breakfast bar, Hammond could see the old clock tower through the arched double doors leading to the garden, where a ginger tabby had perched itself on the neighbouring wall. Hammond dismounted his stool at the breakfast bar, took a small chunk of cheese off his plate, and wandered outside the double doors. He offered the morsel to the cat. It bumped its head into his palm and sniffed a few times before tentatively grasping it with its teeth and nibbled whilst remaining on the wall

Hammond chuckled and surveyed his garden. He expanded his chest in a satisfied intake of fresh air and exhaled slowly. He loved his new home. There was still a lot to do to make it perfect, but it was ready for inspection. He admired his new pizza oven that he had set up on the patio. Citronella candles had been placed in tall bamboo torches and spaced apart in a semi-circle that surrounded the new seating area he had made with wooden pallets and cushions.

The laurel hedging around the perimeter of the garden gave absolute privacy, but enabled the sea breeze to filter through the shrubbery. Hammond had debated whether to construct a brick fire pit, but had decided against it, imagining that if he were to have a dog soon, he didn't want to risk it having an injury. But, for now, he was satisfied, and he imagined Alice would be impressed by his efforts.

There were still several boxes waiting to be unpacked. Hammond took his coffee into the sitting room and considered where he would place items to make the room look cosier. He needed to buy more furniture, but he was thrilled with his new turntable – a walnut veneered, manual, two-speed belt drive. It was pricey but a luxury that Hammond intended to use to its fullest potential. Whilst some would prefer a high definition television, Hammond liked nothing better than to drown himself in music, preferring the richness of sound that only an analogue recording on vinyl could produce. Even the occasional crackle or static created a sense of sentimentality.

Two days previously, Hammond had registered with a new GP and had been reassured that his health was adequate. He had no need to worry about making any decisions on life-prolonging medication, despite his secret fears. His headaches and fatigue were likely to be caused by low blood pressure – the stress of work and the lack of hydration being the likely culprits – but his symptoms could be relieved by avoiding alcohol and remembering to stay hydrated. Now that he was retired, the stress levels would undoubtedly reduce, the Doctor had predicted with such positivity that Hammond felt he had been given a new lease of life.

His relief was such that he wandered into Deal town and bought several second-hand books from Oxfam and found a second-hand vinyl store. Enthused like a child in a confectionery shop, he had selected titles that had previously contributed to his former eclectic collection. He had spent over two hundred pounds by the time he had left the shop, but was delighted with his purchases. Many of the album covers were not as pristine as his own former collection had been, but the vinyl's themselves were scarcely scratched.

He selected a second-hand record that he had purchased especially for the occasion of midday unpacking – Jimi Hendrix's *Band of Gypsies* was the prelude for an afternoon of nostalgia. There were several other titles waiting their turn, each album propped up against the leg of the armchair. He emitted a contented sigh as the fusion of blues and funk drifted across the room, and took a swig of coffee before arranging his new books on the bookshelves nestled amongst built-in, oak panelled cupboards. The titles were varied, ranging from classical to modern literature; history books, including local history of the surrounding areas where he was now a resident; and several titles from popular science.

A hard-backed memoir of forensic pathology was Hammond's current evening entertainment. It wasn't directly involved with police detection, but it was close enough. It would take a while for Hammond to think like a retired civilian rather than a former detective, and this was just a way of easing him towards a future focus on gardening or National Heritage sites.

Satisfied with partially-filled shelves, Hammond turned to his other new purchases: a cherry wood, leather top, two-drawer cabinet and matching desk. He had been inspired by the furniture he had seen at Mischa Taylor's house. This furniture was not extravagant, but the items shared a beautiful oxblood finish and looked perfect underneath the small arch window in the far corner.

Hammond sat cross-legged on the floorboards and arranged documents in their individual files. There were the usual certificates, receipts, insurance papers, and HMRC letters, informing him of his new tax code. He rummaged to the bottom of the box and found an old box file previously stored on his wardrobe shelf. He studied the file, running his hand along the top, contemplating it, recognising the scrawl of his former DCI Lloyd Harris. Hammond was fully aware of the contents, but chose not to remind himself of the associated upset that he would inevitably feel if he read through the contents of an old case he had investigated ten years previously. Instead, he dismissed it, hiding it away in the desk cupboard, and continued with his filing.

*

Alice arrived on the dot of 6.30pm, her timing so accurate that Hammond wondered if she had waited up the road until the minute had struck. His front door was open before she had left the car. She radiated a vivacious demeanour, dressed in a sunshine yellow skirt and pristine white t-shirt, smiling a greeting as she carefully carried a white potted orchid. Alice offered him the plant before accepting his friendly kiss on the cheek, and stepped inside the porch.

'It smells lovely in here,' she exclaimed as she followed him into the glassed gallery that led into the open kitchen.

'That's the beeswax polish,' Hammond shyly uttered the obvious. He had made the home look as comfortable and dressed as he could. The furniture polish had added to the mixed aromas of the fresh herbs he had potted on the windowsill and the citronella oil that was wafting in through from the back garden.

Alice stopped in one spot as she admired the surroundings. 'Oh wow!' She turned around to face Hammond, her hands clasped in front of her chest as she exclaimed her excitement for him. 'This is amazing!'

Alice almost skipped as he led her from one room to the next, pointing out the original fireplace, the sweeping staircase that led to the first floor, and then, as his *pièce de résistance,* he took her through the arch doors into the garden. The pizza oven was prepped and ready, the escaping heat creating refraction shimmers that danced with the flickering candles.

The summer evening was still light, but the scene was homely and romantic. Hammond couldn't wipe the grin off his face even if he had been asked to.

*

The evening was the most pleasurable time Hammond had enjoyed for years. His handmade pizza had been a success; even he admitted it was better than he had tasted previously. He didn't mention that Alice's company had added to the enjoyment, although he thought it.

The two of them had eaten until they were uncomfortably swollen. Hammond was tipsy and merry, Alice enthusing over his good fortune to have such a lovely home. Their awkwardness had gone, and they chatted with such ease as they reclined in the garden that it was as if they were not relative strangers at all.

Hammond mentioned his desire to have a dog, but he was unsure whether to buy a puppy or to go searching for an animal wanting re-homing. Both ideas had their advantages, he mused.

'I've always liked the idea of re-homing personally,' Alice said. 'But you may not know its true history, so you won't know for sure what you are taking on.'

'Surely that's like any relationship,' Hammond suggested.

Their eyes met over their wine glasses, then quickly Alice lowered her gaze and continued her consideration. 'Yes, but if you are going to have a grandchild running around in the near future, you need to be sure that the dog won't attack them or get jealous easily.'

Hammond nodded. 'True. At least if I train a puppy, I can make sure that it knows how to behave around a child.'

Alice rearranged herself on the cushions, the action indicative of her increasing confidence around him. The air was cooling but it was still pleasantly warm. 'Weren't you considering taking on Elijah Johnson's dog at one time?'

'Charlie? Yes, I did, but Mischa took him on whilst she is on bail. Now that we know Elijah will make a full recovery, chances are she'll hand Charlie back when Elijah returns home.'

Alice was quiet for a while as she sipped from her glass. 'What do you think is likely to happen to her?' she asked quietly.

'Well, I'm not expecting her to get a prison sentence, but if she does, it will be a short one. Elijah is standing by her, and that will give a good impression to the jury.'

Hammond studied Alice. She was looking down at her hands, but her mind was occupied.

'Why did you not tell Elijah how you felt about him?' Hammond asked as sensitively as he could.

She looked up, embarrassed. 'Is it that obvious?' she half laughed.

Hammond nodded but didn't elaborate.

Alice sighed. 'Elijah was in a relationship. It wouldn't have been appropriate.'

Hammond took a long sip of his wine, noting it tasted unpleasantly warm. He put the glass down. 'That was what Mischa thought Elijah would have said, had he known she was married.'

'Well, you know what they say about great minds...' Alice smiled and shifted her position, as she deliberately steered the topic of conversation away from herself. 'The news reports didn't mention anything about a vigilante group, but one of the customers at the library said that the man who was arrested for abducting Elijah was a vigilante.'

Hammond cocked his head to one side and gave Alice a mock foreboding look.

'Let's just say Elijah's abduction was not part of a vigilante exposé.'

Alice understood his reluctance to say too much, but she was interested. 'What are your views on vigilante groups, though? Speaking as a police officer? Some countries actually encourage them.'

Hammond was encouraged by Alice's interest and he enjoyed the prospect of an intellectual debate.

'Well, speaking as a *former* police officer, I can say that the act of vigilantism is not supported by English law enforcement officials. The encouragement you are referring to is for a different kind of community-driven law enforcement, where volunteers in communities work together to patrol the streets and monitor any criminal activity. In that sense, citizens do sometimes intervene so to speak, before the Police take action. But it is not the same as these vigilante groups that hunt paedophiles and trap them in stings. Whilst the Police share the concerns of online vigilante groups and individuals who want to expose potential child sex offenders, for example, the actions taken by so-called "paedophile hunters" can be extremely problematic and can create more problems than they solve.'

'What kind of problems?'

'Well…' Hammond shifted his position as he thought of an example without wanting to appear patronising. 'Voluntary vigilantes are not usually trained in the same way a police officer would be, and this could impede a current police investigation. It could alert the offender that they are being monitored and they'd delete evidence that would prevent a conviction.'

'Ok, but there must have been a time when you have known someone to be guilty of something but not been able to charge them?'

Hammond nodded. 'Unfortunately, yes, that has happened a few times.'

'But surely you feel angered about that?'

Hammond considered for a while. He was thinking of several cases over the years where he had not been able to either prevent a crime nor bring the perpetrators to be held accountable.

'I believe that the guilty have to answer to their own consciences eventually,' he said quietly.

'Like karma?'

Hammond looked at Alice and smiled wryly. 'Yes, like karma.'

Alice stayed for several hours, and after she had left, Hammond found himself hoping it would not be too long a wait until she visited him again. He occupied himself collecting the glasses from the patio, and blew out the candles before locking the doors and washing up. Now that Alice had gone, the house seemed very large and quiet. Too quiet.

He found himself heading back to the sitting room where he selected another vinyl, deciding on a Pink Floyd classic, and sat back in his armchair. The vintage single malt that Lois Dunn had bought Hammond to celebrate his birthday was sublime and he savoured every sip, allowing it to pool on his tongue before swallowing. It went against the doctor's orders, but Hammond considered that being teetotal would need a complete absence of alcohol in the house, so it made sense to finish up what remained first. He allowed his head to rest on the back of the chair as the music drifted over him, but he found he couldn't relax.

There was a niggle within him that needed to be acknowledged.

Eventually, Hammond got up from the chair and sought the box file that he had hidden in his desk hours previously. He returned to the chair, letting the file rest on his lap for a minute, then he opened it, fingering the assortment of photographs and notes that Lloyd Harris had written years before.

Ten years earlier, his former DCI Harris had requested Hammond look into a series of suspicious suicides. The investigation had led him to Patricia Goodchild – a woman who had taken several young people under her wing with the sole purpose of using them as pawns in her criminal dealings and, for some, encouraging them to take their own lives.

The malt was helping to take the edge off, but the grief over the death of his former DCI Lloyd Harris and Detective Sergeant Galvin was resurfacing in his chest. Maybe it was what Alice had said, or maybe the recent meeting with Anne Galvin had triggered the start of his review, but there was an itch that needed to be scratched.

The murders of both men had not yet been truly resolved. Whilst their attacker, Bradley Kelsey, had been apprehended and incarcerated for his crimes, the one who had been truly responsible, the one who had instigated numerous crimes against many trafficked and vulnerable victims as well as himself and his colleagues, was Patricia Goodchild. She was a woman of incapacitated conscience, the closest example of a sociopath that Hammond had encountered throughout his career. If there was true justice, she would have been incarcerated for life, but instead she had faked her own death and absconded.

Hammond poured another shot of the malt, but this time he threw it down his throat, wanting to dull the anger rising within him. Maybe Stadden had a point; maybe suffering was the only language that Goodchild would understand. Even if she had been incarcerated, chances were she would have manipulated her fellow inmates to commit atrocities, just like she did all those who had followed her in the past.

He wondered where she was now. Probably living in luxury, feeding off the suffering of many more. People like her couldn't stop hurting others.

Hammond was beginning to get drunk, but he was rational.

A thought emerged. Hammond wasn't a police officer any more, so he was effectively free to do as he wished. Maybe this was his opportunity to scratch that one itch whilst he could do something about it. He sat up straighter in the chair, the thoughts becoming clearer in his mind. No-one would have to know. If he investigated Goodchild's whereabouts privately, then all he would have to do would be to point the Police in the right direction.

A few years earlier, a colleague had described Hammond as a man who worked like a dog after a bone. He kept digging until he got a resolution. And as Hammond thought about it, he realised the man had been right. He could not fully relax into retirement until he found closure.

I'm going to do it, thought Hammond. *I'm going to find that bone and dig it up for good.*

*

AUTHOR'S NOTE

The background of this novel is based on the work of law enforcement officers of Kent Police and the Kent and Essex Major Crime Directorate. It is a work of fiction that has been loosely based on procedures and investigations, but it is not intended to portray realistic events or investigations that have taken place in Kent Police's history.

The location of this novel has been based in South East Kent, in the United Kingdom. Although real locations have been described, fact and fiction have been intertwined, as have some of the historic events associated with these locations. Whilst I can confirm that there is a disused munitions storage chamber hidden in the banks of Hythe Canal, the descriptions of the connecting tunnels are fictitious.

This is a work of fiction, so the names of characters, some places and timings, are not authentic.

C.D. Neill
May 2020